Calico Jam

JOANNE GREENE

ISBN
978-1-959314-46-2 (Paperback)
978-1-959314-47-9 (eBook)
978-1-959314-45-5 (Hardcover)

Apologia

Some conversations and remembrances spring whole and alive to the memoirist. Others have to be reconstructed and remembered, renewed. with the patchwork result that pays more service to a subjective private truth that to cold reality. Memory is often at the mercy of vagaries and impulses not always of a person's understanding. Like a solitary woman rearranging the furniture of her home so that she might have a refreshed view of her life, our memories can be rearranged and replaced, converting them to soothing deceivers, tools for personal survival.

The settings and locations are real: some alien names, as close as remembrance brings them, have stayed with me whether or not I ever had the privilege of a visit or hospitality within their boundaries.

The characters who populate this tale have been assembled from scraps scavenged from collective and individual memories. They are as real or unreal as you like.

Some stories are true, and some stories are not true. This story is both.

Book One

"…. with mingled affection and disgust…."

Calico jam,
The little Fish swam
Over the Syllabub Sea.
He took off his hat
To the Sole and the Sprat,
And the Willeby-Wat:
But he never came back to me;
He never came back,
He never came back,
He never came back to me

They had lived serenely and confidently in a community so circumscribed and circumspect that its members projected the message that here were at last, the Chosen People. The emphatic canon of the family and those of their social, economic and business acquaintance was that they knew somehow that were was life out there in the rest of the world, but couldn't imagine how to relate to it and why they should have to. Successful old and established families lived in polite proximity without exciting any abrasive or intrusive contact. Their lives, ostensibly independent, were bound in a network of impersonal interdependence to common institutions and belief systems. Even those old families that had lost their fortunes modest or considerable to the Wall Street debacle, as my great-grandfather called it, maintained a frosty aloofness, easing the edge of panic with the childlike belief that someday they would regain their wealth, social and political positions and board seats when the Republicans returned to save the country.

Some of these fortunes were regained or rebuilt; ours was not.

My cousin Ralph called her "Gramma" and Aunt Jeanette called her "Nanny". When I was very small, I decided to make her my own and call her "Nammy". Aunts and uncles, cousins, mother and father corrected, teased, cajoled and threatened me for my determined bid for individuality and claim to the lovely mother of my mother. I held fast, compressing my lips and rolling my eyes. She remained all my life: "Nammy."

I came to spend my summers with Nammy at Edgecombe when I was about eleven years old. It had been arranged that after completion of my spring term at St. Anne's School for Girls where I boarded. I would be put on the train for the farm upstate. At the end of the summer, I returned to school. For holidays or unforeseen emergencies, I stayed with my Great Uncle Clifford and Aunt Evelyn at their home in New Jersey.

It seems odd and extravagant that we called Edgecombe a farm. Nammy had a large garden fenced in against the intrusion of the deer, some wooded land with a pond and brook; it could hardly have been called a farm. I think that compared to our mundane north-Jersey lives, encompassed as they were by the muffled roar and muted glow of Manhattan beyond the cliffs, and clotted with houses and traffic, it followed that we considered this upstate preserve, so far from our suburban congestion, a "farm".

For the most part, our family Diaspora extended to an area encompassed by a day or two of back-road driving to the Jersey Pine Barrens or upstate New York in the Catskills and Adirondacks. A member's departure from the family circle was usually prompted by what was apprehended by the reigning patriarch and his consort as inappropriate behavior or, as it later came to be called generations hence: "lifestyle". Judgment was pronounced, or perhaps discretely whispered, and the offending member departed for Cahoonzie, Thendara, Ong's Hat or Manahawken to establish a romantic, rustic and utterly seductive oasis far from the barren waste of middle-class conformity.

In casual conversation, the children called Edgecombe "the farm", avoiding personalizing the home to which Nammy had willingly exiled herself, anticipating her disfavor and perhaps attempting to alleviate the anxiety and anger engendered by a fall from grace. The disapproval of the family was strong, but as time passed, this interdiction did not extend to out-and-out shunning and the children were grudgingly permitted to spend some small portion of their summers with Nammy; not from any easing of their censure, but rather in an uneasy avoidance of giving truthful answers to the questions of their curious young about why she lived so far away and why she no longer came to family gatherings.

Edgecombe was my refuge and sanctuary.

Edgecombe and Nammy.

Ardath had given me a journal the first summer I came to stay at Edgecombe. I was thrilled and touched by her gesture, but I don't think she gave it to me out of any affection. She did feel sorry for me; perhaps pity would be a better word. For a girl only two years my senior, she affected an air of lofty superiority. She really did seem much older, and never let me forget the enormous disparity in our ages and my unsettled place in the family. My discomfort and awe were occasionally swept away by her lavish attention and care, only too soon afterward to be replaced by cold, withering scorn. I learned to accept the pain of this rejection because it had been my close companion for as long as I could remember and I adored her and her brother as only a lonely child could.

Ardath and Cameron were the twin children of Nammy's brother Clifford. I believed them to be the most beautiful and accomplished people in the world. My puppyish adoration must have been quite comical and annoying, and I can now understand their exasperation with me. I tagged along after them chattering incessantly. They would contrive to shake their unwanted acolyte by means ingenious and occasionally cruel, sometimes abandoning me in the middle of a game designed to occupy and amuse us on a long summer afternoon. After hiding for what seemed hours in a hot, rank privy or chill, moss-padded spring house. I would emerge, fighting back the tears and hurry to the kitchen where

Nammy was making tea and scones. I would hug her fiercely from behind and yell at her for expressing surprise and concern for my anguish. Momentarily purged of my rage and pain, I would saunter past the dining room table where Ardath and Cam bent their shining heads over a jigsaw puzzle with counterfeit intensity, snickering and humming, mocking my stupidity. I'd studiously ignore them, and wait for them to forget their cruelty, which they always did, and with cool alacrity to welcome me again to their charmed circle.

Occasionally I would join Alonzo in his shop behind the house where he made woodcarvings for the tourists who sometimes passed the farm on their way to the upper lakes. Alonzo was always kind and amusing. He seemed to be comfortable with children and was never short or impatient. I was careful not to touch any of his tools and kept reverent silence while he worked. His thick brown hands, flat nailed and scarred moved deftly, choosing the exact chisel or knife he needed. I wondered how he had ever cut himself, he seemed to do it so easily.

"Hello, Alonzo."

"Hello, little one. Whatcha doin'?

He looked up at me from the fish he was carving and smiled.

"Nothing."

I stretched my arms behind my back and sighed.

"Nothin'? He leaned toward me, fist on hip. "Nobody never does nothing'?"

I laughed happily, and he joined me. He always made me feel better, although I never quite knew why.

"Is that an Indian saying?" I asked.

"Oh yeah! Another heap big wise Indian saying!" He struck a pose, looking up into the middle distance, through the rusting corrugated wall and slowly raised his left arm. "Heap big wise Indian saying number forty-seven, under heading 'How to Dazzle Paleface Tourists in Three Easy Lessons!'"

We both laughed hugely.

He turned back to his carving.

Alonzo Two Feathers was a Mohawk Indian from somewhere east of the mountains near the Hudson Valley. In his youth he had been a high-steel man working on the skyscrapers of Manhattan and Brooklyn. He was retired on disability while still in his prime and moved upstate with Nammy. Here he scraped a tenuous living doing odd jobs for the tradesmen in town, acting as guide for fishermen and hunters from the city, and creating wood carvings for the tourist trade. "Made in the Adirondaks, USA by American Indian Craftsmen." was burnt into the bases of his imaginative work. Tales and fancies from his multifaceted history entertained and riveted his young audiences, seasoned as they were with Algonquin and Mohawk place names, Yiddish expressions and aphorisms acquired during the time spent in Manhatten.

"Why were you in the sky?" I had asked years earlier when I first met him. He had told me he had fallen from the sky like Sky Woman, who was caught and borne up by a flock of geese flying beneath the hole in heaven.

"I worked in the sky!" he bragged, puffing out his chest.

Alonzo bent forward, confidingly. I settled back on Nammy's rocker, tired and happy, waiting for his story.

"Many, many moons ago," he began in a low, serious voice, "I worked on the high steel", he pointed "... up in the sky!" I gave a satisfying gasp.

"Me and many other Mohawk worked on the buildings. White men were afraid to go up there. They were afraid of falling!' He laughed at the absurdity of such a fear. I joined him. We laughed long, before he continued, warming to his small sleepy audience of one.

"One day," he dropped his voice and paused dramatically. "I was catching hot rivets in my can. like this:" he demonstrated, swinging his arms around, catching the unseen white-hot metal in the unseen funnel, retrieved it with his unseen pincers and riveted it into the unseen beam, swaying all the time over the unseen abyss below. He stopped. I was sitting on the edge of the rocker, holding my breath, eyes wide.

"Then, you know what happened?" Alonzo's face was close to mine, his black eyes shining, his breath pungent.

"What?" I could hardly speak.

"I was workin', not paying attention, when all of a sudden ..."
I couldn't bear it.

"What what what!!!" I was almost in tears.

"This great big monkey come around the back of the building, says 'Get out of my way, redskin, we're makin' a movie here!' And he swing his big hairy arm around, like this ..." he demonstrated, swooping down then up, then windmilling, eyes wide, staggering backward. "Then he knock me clean off the beam I was standin' on and down I went! Fifty stories I fell! Had to pick me up in a basket, they did!"

He had started to laugh, booming and hooting, and at first didn't hear my cries. It took my mother, father and Nammy to calm me down and to tuck me into Nammy's trundle bed and an uneasy sleep. Alonzo was not soon forgiven by the disapproving adults, but I had forgiven him by the next day. and wanted to hear more about the monkey. Sky Woman and the turtle on whose back we all lived.

That was my first trip to Edgecombe.

My father had driven my mother, Toby and me all the way from Palisades to the farm in the old station wagon. Toby had been sick. He was little, only about two or three, and he slept and cried a lot when he wasn't throwing up. My mother wasn't happy about going and had sat with silent, compressed lips for most of the journey.

We arrived at dusk, bumping up the long rutted, rocky drive. I craned my neck for a glimpse of my grandmother. I bounced and jabbered continually, to the intense annoyance of my mother whose rebukes fell on deaf ears. Nammy was waiting on the porch, smiling and waving a little, sort of shyly. I was out of the car before it stopped and jumped into her waiting arms.

The doors of the station wagon slowly opened and disgorged the rest of its wilted passengers who stiffly moved towards the woman who had left them years earlier for the north and a crippled red man.

"Hello, Eleanor, you're looking well!" Nammy, still clasping me against her apron, reach out her free arm to embrace her daughter.

Eleanor offered her cheek. "Mother." she said.

"Come in and have something to eat, you must be starving. That was a long trip." Nammy smiled her welcome. She continued to hold me against her as she led the way through the front room to the kitchen.

I was too intoxicated with excitement and joy to notice anything but the loveliness of my grandmother's home. The house was warm and ambient with the smells of baking, herbs and spices, melted candles and fresh linen. A grandfather clock clucked in the lofty hall, its aged face gazing magisterially through the arch into the parlor where a stuffed pheasant perched on a scarred sideboard. The living and dining rooms were cluttered with heavy old pine and oak, with piles of books overflowing from bookcases that seemed to line the walls of every room. A frowzy, scarred tiger cat briefly looked up from his perch on the top of an old upright piano, turned away and resumed his interrupted nap. I was called back from my wanderings by the voice of my mother urging me to return to the kitchen for something to eat.

In the kitchen, my grandmother hurried between the ice box and the table, putting out bread and butter, cold meat, cheese and fruit. My father ate steadily and politely, my mother picked delicately at a small plate arranged with bread and cheese. Toby was dozing in her arm, clutching a bit of apple, browning in his sticky hand. I suddenly felt unwell, and slipped away from the table, away from the dim light and buzzing hum of restrained conversation, needing to continue my interrupted tour.

I found my way into the parlor where Alonzo sat with his feet up on a needlework footstool, scratching a big drowsy dog behind the ears. A cigarette dangled from the corner of his mouth and he was reading the New York Daily News. He looked up at me and smiled.

"Where did *you* come from?" I asked with the shameless curiosity of the very young.

That's when he told me that he came from the sky.

I woke the next day to a brilliantly sunny morning, full of the warm haze and sharp commanding air of the mountains. Ignoring the protestations and admonitions of the adults, I took Toby by the hand and showed him around the garden and fields. Already feeling proprietary, I gave my little brother a tour, grandly pointing to the far peaks, the humming pines and silent pond.

"And this is Nammy's, too." I informed him, as I pulled him stumbling and mewing beside me. How wonderful it would be to live here! How beautiful and exciting! The weather was conspiratorially gorgeous and I decided that I would stay forever and ever, whatever my parents and brother decided to do. Toby's guided tour was interrupted when he began to whine and drag at my hand.

"Potty, Jo. Need potty." I looked back at him, exasperated. His bright hair shone in the sun; with his free hand he rubbed his eyes and put his finger in his nose. Sighing mightily, I acquiesced.

I bent over and whispered "You can pee behind this tree, Toby, it's alright!"

He shook his head fiercely. "No, no. Mama spank!"

"Toby! I won't tell! Honest injun!" I laughed and raised my hand.

"The boy will tell. Mama will spank!"

I gave him an impatient shake. "Nobody will tell! Nobody will see!"

"Boy will see!" he insisted, pointing behind me. By now Toby was clutching himself and starting to cry. I turned.

There *was* a boy. I was startled, shocked by this intrusion into our idyllic day.

"Who are you?" I called.

The boy was small, clad in tiny faded overalls, and appeared to be around Toby's age. The child's skin was bronzed, his dark hair lighted by the sun. He stood silently leaning against a tree, staring at us with round, black eyes.

"WHO ARE YOU? DON'T YOU KNOW THIS IS PRIVATE PROPERTY? WHAT ARE YOU DOING HERE?" I shouted.

The boy turned, quick as a deer and ran back through the wood, so swiftly that for a frightening moment, I thought I had seen a spirit.

I turned back to Toby. As I opened my mouth to speak, I noticed that he had wet his pants.

My mother had yelled at us both and swept my brother away to change his clothes. I didn't mention our encounter with the child in the woods and the incident was forgotten until teatime, when I noticed a station wagon pull up the driveway. It sat idling for a minute or so, the dust rising golden around it. Then I saw Alonzo leaning on his cane as he walked from the back of the house holding the little boy by the hand. He led the child to the car and helped him into the back seat. Alonzo then bent down and said a few words to the driver, nodded and waved as the car backed out of the yard. My mother and father were seated with their backs to the window tending to the tea and making polite comments. I looked at Nammy. She was busy cutting and distributing slices of cake. I opened my mouth to speak, then stopped as though tongue-tied. I think at that moment some tiny bubble surfacing from a deep instinctive well stopped me from asking the question. Then again, maybe I didn't know what to say. Besides, I had been taught never to interrupt adults under pain of banishment from the company. As it turned out, it didn't matter; it was already too late.

The next afternoon, determined to find the source of the creek which bordered the farm, I embarked on a solitary adventure, seduced by the magic power of the tumbling water, the hills shouting down the wind, the buzzing, lambent air, and my joy. I lost all track of time. So many discoveries greeted me: a nest of rabbits, squirming in their own little cave of leaves and grass; a pair of red squirrels, angry at my intrusion beneath their home, flung pine cones at me and shrilled indignantly; a bird that scampered up the side of a tree and purred in surprise; carpets of flowers entertaining huge congregations of bees and butterflies; a darting dragonfly perched on a blade of cattail grass, his jeweled eyes reflecting the undulant shine of the pond beneath. Only the earthy nagging reminder of a meal missed turned me back, laced with welts and scratches from ambushing nettles and blackberry canes and swollen with mosquito bites. I raced toward the house, glowing and euphoric.

I returned overflowing with happiness, bursting to tell everyone of my discoveries and brimming with questions. A shock awaited me.

Mother spoke coldly as I ran joyfully from the glowing sunshine into the cool, shaded room. "Get your things, Joanna, we're leaving."

My heart sank and I felt as if my heart would break. "NO!"

I hadn't noticed Nammy, who was standing near the door. She came quickly to me and bent down. She took my hands in hers, forcing a smile. "You need to go home now dear. You can come to visit me again sometime if you want!"

"That remains to be seen!" my mother harshly interrupted. "There doesn't seem to be any reason to come back."

Nammy straightened and stuffed her hands in her apron pockets, turning towards her daughter. She began to speak and changed her mind. She looked away, shaking her head. My heart was broken and I felt that all life and joy were gone. I broke into tears. Through the mist of my anguish, I vaguely saw my father, his face blotched, mutely pulling a shirt on my squirming, wailing brother, and Alonzo, turning quickly to leave the room. So enraptured had I had been by the warmth, comfort and beauty that surrounded and accompanied Nammy wherever she went, whatever she did, I couldn't see how strained and painful the atmosphere had become.

On the way home I sulked and cried. I believed I would never see Nammy and her beautiful home again. I was to be imprisoned in our ugly house in New Jersey, surrounded by noisy traffic and crying children, dusty trees and stinging air. I mused with stubborn self-pity about the wonders lost to me forever. Would the baby bunnies be caught and eaten by the fusty one-eyed cat that slept on the piano? Did the silent little boy know about the bee tree, the tiny orange salamanders in the creek, or the owl's nest and at the base of its tree, the soft little packages of tiny bones?

My tears exhausted and my throat aching, I dozed fitfully, fatigued by my rage and sorrow. Little dreams and fancies flitted in and out as my sleep skimmed back and forth, like surf at the beach. In one dream I ran with Toby and the little dark boy across Nammy's meadow to the pond. There were white ducks and brown chickens running with us and flowers everywhere. I heard my mother's voice far away: "Be careful . . . be careful Toby, Toby, who is that? That little creature, so black . . . be careful." The voice faded away and I ran into the cold water of the pond, followed by the little ones: I wasn't afraid; I was happy. My mother's voice grew louder and I awoke with a start to find the light almost gone, heavy traffic roaring around us.

"If I had known, we wouldn't have gone. Oh Toby! He's throwing up again. Hand me that face cloth, hurry."

My father murmured something and my mother snapped back at him, her voice heavy with scorn.

"Come *on*! Bad Enough she went with him! That was bad enough! A woman of her age! How could she! NO! I didn't know.

Nobody told me. None of them ever told me." She dabbed fiercely at Toby's febrile cheeks as he loudly protested her ministrations.

"Mother," I interrupted a fresh new bout of righteous pique. "I think I'm going to puke."

Months passed and my youthful resilience healed the wounds incurred at that painful visit. I thought about Nammy and her home with nostalgic pangs, like a memory dredged up to commemorate blissful times gone forever. I told my friends and schoolmates, with some embroidery and romance, of the beautiful farm of my grandmother, far, far away in the northern mountains. I tried writing to her, to keep her alive in myself. After what seemed like a long interval, I finally received a note card from her that had a picture of a sun bonneted girl watering flowers and a line thanking me for the visit and signed: love. I cried and shouted at her absent sweetness and determined to hate her and forget her completely.

In our family, Sundays and holidays were spent visiting family and social acquaintances. On major holidays such as Christmas and Easter, we made obligatory appearances at Great-Grandfather Ashburn's house, just a few blocks from our home in Palisades. Faithful observance of these visits had been mandated by some higher authority, lost in history; something like the handing down of the Tablets of the Law. Entertaining even the remotest thought of other plans or activities on these occasions would have been unthinkable; it simply wasn't done.

Thanksgiving was celebrated at Uncle Clifford's home in Fort Lee. Uncle Cliff and Aunt Evelyn lived in a rather gloomy, sprawling house just a block or so from the palisades which fell sheer to the river and faced uptown Manhattan. The house, aptly called Cliff House, had undoubtedly seen better days. At one time it served as the residence of a wealthy New York family who lived there when it had been a more exclusive address, as yet unincroached upon by the rising tide of immigrants and minor mafiosi fleeing from the rumbling threat of social reform and its inevitable concomitant purges of the city's depravity. The house is gone now; torn down along with many other grand old houses to make way for high rise apartments and the offices of multinational conglomerates. The veneer and quirky personality of the area once defined by the exclusivity and arrogance of old money was gone forever.

I had looked forward to the holiday. Here was to be a feast fulsomely lavish enough to feed the entire state of New Jersey. Besides the grandest turkey in the history of the world, this traditional meal included many overcooked vegetables and garnishes too numerous to count, providing an unimpeachable excuse for not eating succotash or turnips: there simply wasn't enough room on the plate.

We were always late arriving at these gatherings and a subtle pall of reproof hung about us as we entered. Mother apologized abjectly, blaming unruly children and lost gloves. She never seemed to relax and enjoy these events, and my own relief from her reproving eye was to lose myself in the crowd. Ardath and Cameron were there, surrogate hosts to the younger children. That day Ardath was especially exuberant, greeting us all with hugs, pinches and insults, enveloping us in a lively comradeship blessed by her grace and energy. She led us all off, Cameron by her side. He tossed laughing insults at his sister: Bully! Miss Bossy! Ardath ignored him and ran ahead of us up the staircase to the gallery where hung dim, fumed oil paintings of hunt scenes and naval battles.

"We're going to play hide and seek! Ralph, you're IT. Shut up, Ralph. Joanna you have to go with Toby, he's too little to hide by himself. Shut UP, Ralph! The first person back gets a prize and if anybody sees the ghost and screams Cam will hang him or her over the gallery rail by his or her feet. Michael stop jumping around, you look like a puppet. Those are the rules, to be obeyed OR ELSE. *Do you all understand?*"

We boiled around her in a fever of excitement, determined to be the first Home and not to scream when we saw the ghost. I hurried with Toby, hissing strict orders for him to be quiet and glancing over my shoulder at Ralph, shoulders hunched resentfully, forehead pressed to the wall.

"Fsven, fate, fifnine, SIXTY! S'one, stoo, s'three . . ."

I began to panic and pushed open the first door I came to. We hurried into the room and I closed the door quietly. We had entered a bedroom, unmistakably feminin. The smell of baking turkey that had swirled around us since our arrival was replaced by a flowery, powdery, lady smell, permeating everything, clinging, wafting. I moved curiously around the room, glancing back occasionally at Toby, who still stood with his finger against his mouth, shushing wetly for silence. I smiled and gave him the OK sign to signal my approval.

The dresser was cluttered with pots and jars of creams and unguents. There were rainbow faceted perfume bottles, some with towering glass stoppers, others with little bulbs that hissed florid bouquets into the air. The air stung; I sneezed.

"SHHHH!" Toby sibilated behind me.

I whirled around, bounded over the multi-cushioned bed, and landed in front of him. 'SHHHH!" Toby fell back, laughing and squealing.

'I see Joanna-and-Toby one-two-three!" Ralph had thrown open the door and triumphantly whirled around to run back home to tag us out. Before he got to base, however, Cameron, sashaying with an exaggerated swagger, reached out before him and smacked the wainscotting.

"Home free all! Alley, alley, in free!"

Shouts and howls reverberated down the gallery.

"NO FAIR! NO FAIR!" Ralph, purple-faced, fists clenched, screamed at a laughing Cameron and a calmly poised Ardath.

"YOU should know the rules, Ralphie. You have to be a good sport or we won't invite you to participate in future games!"

Ardath, queenly as ever, flaunting her newly acquired Big Word, ended all protestations.

The yelling continued: Toby squealed and bounced down the stairs on his bottom, Michael cavorted and waved his arms hooting "I'm the ghost! Hoohoohoo! I'm going to get you!", and Ralph crying: "I'm going to tell!", flying before all the tumbling children.

Aunt Evelyn appeared at the bottom of the stairs, blissfully ignoring the chaos. "Children! Wash your hands! Dinner is ready! Come along now!" She turned away toward the kitchen, absently wiping her hands on her skirt. The maelstrom of children braked as they approached the bottom of the stairs, swiftly and silently filing toward the powder room beneath the front stairs, an occasional elbow shooting out to gain or maintain position in the race for first place at the lavatory.

Before claiming our appointed seats, we filed up to pay obeisance to our incredibly ancient great-grandparents Ashburn. They sat in aloof brittle splendor at either side of Uncle Cliff's chair at the head of the table. At the end of the line of homage, I lifted Toby to kiss the dusty parchment cheek of Matilda Whitcomb Ashburn. Toby whined and sniffed, kicking his heels against my stomach. Great-Grandmother Ashburn tilted her head back and regarded this thrice removed issue of her womb through water y cerulean-blue eyes.

"Such a cunning little whelp! So sad! So sad!"

Toby twisted away and I kissed the air in her direction, but she had already turned to Clifford who with linen tucked above his ascot had begun to carve the shinty streaming turkey.

"Remember, Clifford, white meat, white meat and the Pope's nose!"

Dinner was officially about to begin and we placed ourselves obediently around the celebratory board. Aunt Evelyn rapped reprovingly on the table and Clifford, with an apologetic start, put down his carving knife as we bent our heads for grace.

We were situated around the table in an arrangement from which we never deviated, with children seated between their respective parents. Years earlier one of the adults in an attempt to elevate the table talk from the trivial to the scurrilous, suggested that the minor members of the family be relegated to their own table in the sun room. The experiment proved to be a resounding failure; the young being in constant need of reprimands, arbitrations and other sundry disciplines, resulting in the disruption of two tables instead of just one. At subsequent feasts the children were back in their original seats where rebukes and punishments could be meted out more conveniently, and where tedious conversation would henceforth be reinstated.

As dictated by this inviolate tradition, I sat between my mother and father. Toby was in chair with a tray between mother and me. Next to father was Great Aunt Cora, Uncle Cliff's younger sister and beside her was seated Albert, her "gentleman friend" whose hound like countenance and sad eyes appeared apologetically and sometimes uninvited at our family gatherings. Opposite them was Aunt Jeannette, with Ralph between her and Uncle Edward; the parental heads popped up and down in comical unison as they murmured and hissed at their son who was still fuming about his humiliation at the hands of his cousins. Cameron sat on Great-grandfather's right next to my mother, and Ardath sat on Great-grandmother's left. Beside her, looking pretty and just a little smug Aunt Shirley sat, ignoring Michael who perched twitching and mugging between her and her vague, distant husband, my Uncle Timothy.

Presiding at the foot of the table was Great Aunt Evelyn, the author and commander of the feast; the success or failure of which depended upon her decisions and directions. Everlyn was large and imposing, inspiring the indisputable deference accorded the doyenne of the household. But for her friendly, even tender, personal smiles and uncharastically heartily laugh, she would have been truly formidable. Our Great-aunt had gone on to college and had earned an impressive academic degree, later doing post-graduate work at the Sorbonne in Paris. This lofty accomplishment never bore practical fruit but certainly enhanced her social standing. She had met Great

Uncle Clifford through her classmate, Great Aunt Cora, who had introduced him apologetically as: "… My big brother, a confirmed bachelor, and terrible bridge player." Clifford and Evelyn married after several years of "keeping company", much to the surprise of the senior Ashburns, who thought she was much too good for him.

The meal began. The aforementioned excesses of food and drink weighed the table and clashed as we passed bowls, condiments, reached for gravy and sauce boats and searched for the butter. Two caveats were recognized: the baby (in this case Toby) got a drumstick and Great-grandmother Ashburn got the Pope's nose.

The three children of my exiled grandmother bent unperturbed over their meals. My mother, Eleanor, was the eldest and probably resembled her the most physically. Tall and slim, with what was then called "good bones" which gave her profile a patrician cast. There the resemblance stopped, for she tended to be withdrawn, rarely initiating a conversation and slow to respond to others' overtures. That day she attended quietly to her meal, occasionally checking Toby, who happily beat on his tray with his drumstick. Jeannette was my mother's junior by a couple of years, but looked and acted as though she were much younger. She was plumper than my mother and had fair hair that tended to be fly-away, merry hazel eyes and a quick, nervous laugh. That day she swiveled between social exchanges with the rest of the company and the tedious task of remonstrating with Ralph, who sat glowering and kicking at the chair legs as he picked at his food. Shirley was the youngest and prettiest of the three. Her hair was ash blond (Ardath said it was bleached) and her eyes startlingly blue. She was always impeccably groomed and had very long, very red nails. Beside her, Michael ("Next week I'm going to be six-and-a-half") dug into his meal with gusto, briefly and mechanically interrupted by his father who switched his fork from his left hand to his right.

I remember thinking: "Nammy should be here, too. It's so terribly unfair." My memory of her when I was very small, sitting in the chair that now housed my little brother, was one of comfortable happiness. She fed me and cuddled me. I was told much later that she had coached me when I took my first steps and soothed me when I was afraid to go to kindergarten that first fateful day. It was odd that of the few outstanding memories I had were of her, not my mother.

I tried to listen to the adults as they exchanged comments and bits of information, hoping that for once there would be an Interesting comment, a mumbled hint of a scandal or a lurid crime.

"We're going to try to get back to the Fair in the spring, before they close."

"Oh, the crowds were terrible. We stood in line for an hour before we could get into the World of Tomorrow. I got quite faint. I wouldn't go back again for anything."

"Good Heavens! You're eating like a bunch of starving Armenians! Don't your mothers ever feed you?"

"Grandmother is asking for something, what does she want, Clifford?"

"Would someone please pass the cranberry relish?"

"Ralph, don't. Stop picking at your food."

"He was a real loss, the company won't be the same without him. Some problem with his innards, I understand. Incurable."

"Clifford!"

"Well, I want to go back to the fair! Mama wouldn't let us go into the midget village, I couldn't even buy a post card! Next time I'm going in and looking in their little houses."

"Michael look at that mess! Timothy makes him stop mixing his food like that! We're going to put you out on the back stoop if you don't stop eating like an animal, young man!"

"They found something in his gizzard, or bowel somewhere. A growth as big as my fist. Sewed him up and sent him home to die. Poor bugger."

"Clifford! Pas devant les infants!"

"Well, I want to go back to see those naked ladies swimming in that big tank! This kid in my class, his father let him in to see them! They had nothing on!"

"Oh God, don't get up Evelyn, I could use another napkin."

"I don't know how they'll manage without him."

"I hope this weather holds. We're trying to get up to Bear Mountain for a day for one last visit before the weather changes."

"It's the damndable Democrats that's driving us all to perdition! The country is being ruined! All those foreigners and blackamoors. It's getting so you can't walk the streets! Something should be done!"

"Clifford, I think your mother is asking you something."

"I wasn't allowed to go on the rides or see the freaks. Mother didn't want me. I was scared to look at them anyway."

"I saw Charlie McCarthy! He was on a flying carpet!"

"Charee!"

"CharLEY, Toby."

"CharEE!"

We all laughed as Toby wielded his greasy scepter and thumped his tray, scattering peas and bits of potato.

Great-Grandfather continued his diatribe against the Democrats with a litany of all the grievances inflicted on us by that traitor in the White House. No one seemed to pay attention to him, least of all Great-Grandmother who was being served an unprecedented third helping and asking if she ever got the pope's nose. Evelyn politely engaged the uncomfortable Albert in a conversation involving the acquisition of a pair of pheasants for the run behind the house, how difficult it was to get drapes cleaned these days, and so expensive! Albert nodded and murmured mild responses, and Cora ignored him completely.

The covered dishes and platters gradually emptied and the sounds of clattering cutlery and clinking glasses abated. The family, quite sated by the meal, demurring as Aunt Evelyn pressed more food on them, slumped back in their chairs.

The conversation faded into the drowsy afterglow of the day, filtered sun catching the edges of crystal salt shakers and silver bread trays. My ears buzzed and my sleepy eyes watched the company. Michael had become quiescent and was gazing into space, absently wiggling a loose tooth. Aunt Shirley sat with chin in hand smiling mildly at Clifford who was pouring wine and remonstrating mildly with his father, who had become increasingly querulous. My mother stared fixedly at her glass of wine and Evelyn clucked sympathetically at something Great-grandmother was saying. Cameron leaned back in his chair and whispered something to Toby who brightened and began banging on his tray.

"'SERT! 'SERT! 'SERT!" he intoned rhythmically accompanying himself with his bone.

"Good man!" cried Cameron, "I second the motion! It's time for dessert!"

The family began to emerge from the lethargy induced by its earlier overindulgence. Aunt Evelyn rose automatically, continuing to murmur mildly to her mother-in-law, interrupting briefly to call to Edith to start the coffee. Edith, who came in and "did" for my great-aunt brayed compliantly from her post in the kitchen.

Desserts were swept in through the swinging door to a clatter of revived interest and conversation. A devil's food cake topped with foamy white icing, mince and pumpkin pies, a mold of Jello solid with fruits and nuts, and a big bowl of whipped cream for garnishing reburdened the table.

"I want some of each!" Michael lisped through his loosened tooth.

"She should be here!" Great-grandfather shocked me by giving voice to my thoughts. I felt as though I had a stone in my chest.

"Why doesn't she come?"

An immediate uncomfortable silence and an almost imperceptible feeling of retreat diffused the family, like a wave sucking back toward the sea. Before anyone could deflect a new burst of indignation, Great-grandfather began to mumble ominously.

My mother suddenly shifted in her seat, cheeks flaming. She reached for her wine glass and drained it quickly. "I don't think I can eat another bite, Evelyn." She turned to my father, "Ted," she began in a thin voice. Great-grandfather raised his tearful voice as the family stirred and murmured uncomfortably.

"She should be here! This is her family! She should be here out of respect! Not gone away with that goddamn ..."

He was quickly interrupted by Cora and Evelyn who rose simultaneously and in falsely exuberant voices entertained requests for "... desert, coffee or tea and does anyone want an after-dinner drink?" Aunt Evelyn fiercely semaphored to Uncle Cliff who clumsily tried to disarm his inconsolable parent.

"Now Father, you know perfectly well why she doesn't come, after what she did."

This was absolutely the wrong thing to say to Great-grandfather, who began a righteous harangue that ended all hope of realizing a civil conclusion to the holiday. Jeanette stared at him, her mouth open, eyes shimmering; Shirley flung her head back and rolled her eyes. Cora was crying quietly and the children were caught in various states of fascination and confusion. Toby was attempting to squash the remains of his dinner on the tray with his bone. Ralph blinked at his Great-Grandfather in astonishment and Michael had clamped his hands over his mouth, rocking with smothered giggles. Cameron sat straight, lips compressed as though suppressing a smile; Ardath looked strangely detached, examining the wall above our heads.

"We have anisette, cognac, creme-de-menthe, Benedictine ..." Cora chanted, as tears started to course down her cheeks.

"She was my favorite! She should come back ... Oh Annie!"

"I think we'd better go. Jeanette, come on, we'll help clear up."

"CharEE!"

"What in God's name started all that!"

"Sit down, Cora, stop crying!"

"Cora, I've got to leave. I promised my sister I'd stop by. Thank you for having me Evelyn, thanks, Clifford."

"Clifford, take him to the sun room. Bring him a glass of brandy. Good God!"

"I don't understand. it's been ... years!"

"I *knew* this would happen, sooner or later; it was just a matter of time. No, no, Jeanette, Shirley, don't bother with that, Edith and I will tidy up later. Cora, do stop!"

"Well, I think I will have one of those brandies, Evelyn, please."

"You know, I don't think I ever got the Pope's nose. If you find it Evelyn, would you wrap it for me in a bit of waxed paper? I could take it home for lunch. Wonderful, wonderful meal, Evelyn! Everything was just perfect!"

From the sun room came the sounds of grief and helpless, hopeless comforting, an exchange of two men defeated by feelings they feared, unable to connect or understand.

Great Grandmother smiled serenely and gazed across the table at Toby, who was trying to push a pea up his nose. "Dear little tyke! It's all so sad! So sad.

Nothing more was said by our parents about the events of that singular Thanksgiving and we knew not to ask. For our family, normal meant putting up a detached facade and pretending that nothing untoward had happened; it was believed that by ignoring something unpleasant it would go away. The bizarre behavior of our great-grandfather had faded from our minds, much as a case of the chicken pox dwindled and vanished, leaving no memory of their terrible discomfort. All of us, notwithstanding the peculiar circumstances of our upbringing, had much better things to do. Adults were merely necessary functionaries, minions charged with the running of our tidy, unexceptional lives, not seriously charged with feelings and frailties.

That Christmas we went to our Great-grantparent's house for a short visit, just long enough for the exchange of gifts and to sample a spread of food to be taken en buvette, an informality adopted grudgingly only because it had lately gained social approbation. The buffet also imposed on the participant the adventure of finding a place to sit which commanded an adjacent flat surface to accommodate the balanced plates, glasses, flatware and napery, a felicity rarely gained. The subsequent chore of removing and properly disposing of one's china, cutlery and remainders invariably inspired one to beg early withdrawal from the company. Aunt Evelyn, who had gallantly volunteered to act as hostess for her in-laws, rose to the occasion heroically, and seemed as happy to see the back of us as she had been in making us welcome.

The family visit had been uneventful; there hadn't been time to test the emotional climate, only fleeting moments to exchange cordial, occasionally sincere, holiday greetings and wishes for the New Year. Great-grandfather, much diminished since the last time we saw him on Thanksgiving was tucked up in a morris chair with a plaid lap robe over his knees and his slippered feet resting on a little stool. His hands shook and his eyes teared; it was frightening to look at him. Great-grandmother was elegantly dressed in a long chiffon gown and moved slowly through the gathering taking hands, murmuring and smiling a welcome. We all toasted the day, the children with eggnog and the adults with whatever festive drink they chose. The children received gifts from their aunts and we presented Great-grandmother with a poinsettia in a pot wrapped in red foil. Great-grandfather was given a box of monogrammed handkerchiefs. A half-hearted attempt to sing Christmas carols floundered and we were whirled through good-byes in a rather abrupt manner.

As soon as we returned home my mother retired to her room complaining of a headache, leaving Father to get us ready for bed. It was still early and I indignantly asked why I couldn't stay up for a while. Father was struggling with Toby who was working his way into a monumental tantrum and he sternly sent me of to my room.

Christmas night, or as Cam called it: "The Eve of Saint Steve" was strange, burdened with unsettling feelings. For the first time Christmas didn't live up to my expectations. At the same time, I felt guilty for feeling so sad. It must be my own weakness, not the holiday, the tree twinkling with stars, the Christ Child, the caroling and candlelight; everything celebrating joy and fulfillment.

I lay on my bed in the quiet of my room, trying to redeem the day that had turned out to be a such a great disappointment. Tears began to well up and slide hotly down my temples. I felt confined and neglected at the same time. What was wrong? Christmas was supposed to be the best day of the year. I had looked forward to it for months and months. It was certainly true that I didn't get all the things I had asked for; the skates were black and ugly, not gleaming white figure skates like Sonja Henie wore, and why did they give me a doll with a china head? There was a book about the pilgrims; a bottle of bubblebath that smelled like candy; and underwear! You don't give people underwear for a present! My family was dull and Cheap and stupid. Ardath and Cameron had all but ignored me at Great-Grandfather's and the food resembled leftovers: cold and unrecognizable. There was a fruitcake that tasted burnt, a plum pudding, lumpy and sour and warm eggnog with slimy bits in it.

I began to cry aloud in anger and frustration. Sorrowfully I turned over and wiped my nose roughly on the pillow case. There was one consoling memory, the solitary, bright saving moment of the day.

"This is for you, Joanna. From your Grandmother."

I was stunned. My mother held out to me a small box wrapped in bright paper. It was early and chill, she had been kneeling beside the tree distributing gifts and shivering in a light wrap that had been a gift from my father. I stared at the box for a moment, trying to imagine Nammy wrapping it. A homemade card taped to top read: "Dear Jo: I hope you have a very happy Christmas and wonderful New Year." I quickly tore open the box. Inside, wrapped in some tissue was a beautiful blue sweater with little red rosebuds at the buttonholes and around the collar. She had made it herself for me. I pictured her working far into the night, knitting needles flashing and clicking as she sat in her chair in a pool of yellow light cast by the lamp at her side. I felt warmed and content at last. She hadn't forgotten me after all.

Remembering her gift and the fleeting happiness of the morning, I began to cry in earnest. I sat up in my bed and pulled the precious sweater out from under the pillow. Determinedly I pulled it on over my pajamas. At last, I was ready for rest. Clogged with self-indulgent tears I finally fell asleep remembering Nammy and willing myself to dream about being with her at the farm.

This was to be the last Christmas we would be together as a family.

Excerpt from Jo's Journal: June 30th 1940

PERSONAL AND PRIVATE—

THIS JOURNAL IS THE PERSONAL AND PRIVATE PROPERTY OF JOANNA CAROLINE WEBSTER—BORN SEPTEMBER 6TH, 1930 IN THE CITY OF ENGLEWOOD, COUNTY OF BERGEN, STATE OF NEW JERSEY, THE UNITED STATES OF AMERICA, THE CONTINENT OF NORTH AMERICA, THE WESTERN HEMISPHERE, THE EARTH, THE SOLAR SYSTEM, THE UNIVERSE.

ANYONE CAUGHT TOUCHING THIS SECRET, PERSONAL, PRIVATE JOURNAL WILL SUFFER IMMEDIATE TERRIBLE PUNISHMENT.

THIS MEANS YOU!!!!!!!!!!

Ardath and Cameron arrived today at Nammy's to stay for a while. Ardath gave me this journal, which I shall call "Jo's Journal." I was so surprised when she gave it to me, I could have hugged her. She just handed it to me and said something like "Here, Josie, this is for you. It will keep you busy." I couldn't believe it. It will be something like Jo Marsh's journal in "Little Women" (my favorite character in a book). I want to be like Jo, but I don't have any younger sisters to boss around and I have no aptitude for the stage. (Aptitude: meaning talent. I am collecting words for when I grow up and can explain things to people). I could try to boss around Andrew, but it's hard to boss somebody around who doesn't understand what you say, just follows you around. Gives me the creeps. The weather is fine. I am going to stay out of the way until tea and maybe take Andrew down to the pond to catch frogs.

The New Year brought a new decade and a heaving away from the dry spell that was the Great Depression. The new era, reflected in the spirit of the New York World's Fair gave rise to a public optimism not previously entertained in my young life. The social and economic ups and downs characterized by President Roosevelt's first two terms wrenched us into a period of upward acceleration; the ominous rumbles beyond our protective oceans were not seriously regarded. Time moved smoothly, like the dropping away of calendar leaves used to denote the passage of time in movies. The winter gave way to a wet gray spring. But nothing much had changed in my little world.

"What happened to his toes?" Toby was staring at me intently.

"Um, I don't know. I guess they just fell off" I equivocated. "No, wait!" He leaned forward expectantly.

"Here it is:

> *But before he touched the shore, —*
> *The shore of the Bristol Channel,"*

I sat back and raised my voice dramatically.

> *"A sea-green Porpoise carried away*
> *His wrapper of scarlet flannel.*
> *And when he came to observe his feet,*
> *Formerly garnished with toes so neat,*
> *His face at once became forlorn*
> *On perceiving that all his toes were gone!"'*

I finished with a flourish and glanced at my little brother for his reaction. He was frowning.

"How come, how come, because the scarlet flannel, what happened to the, Jo, what's scarlet flannel? What happened to his toes? Did they fall off?" I imagined little thoughts popping around inside his head like the beads on a bagatelle board, ticking back and forth against the little prongs, not falling into the right holes. "What is Porpis, Jo? Is it like a bear? Did the Porpis eat the Pobble's toes?" He looked down at his sandals and wiggled his toes, as if to make sure they were all still there.

"No, Tobiska, a porpoise isn't like a bear, it's like a big fish." I temporized.

He sighed and sat back. "Read that again, Jo."

"No, Toby, I have to do my homework, go play with your toys."

Toby whined and flung himself back on the sofa, rolling about and chanting. "Pobblespobbles, scarlet porpsies, seagreen flannels, toesonose, tobiska, jobo jobiska ...." and fell to the floor with a shout and a laugh.

Toby had run up to me as soon as I had come in the front door. "Read me, Jo, read me!"

I sighed and took the book he held up to me.

"Have you had your snack, Toby?" I asked rashly. He looked at me, round-eyed.

"Uh, NO, NO." This accompanied by a firm shaking of the head. I sighed and fetched milk and cookies from the kitchen. We sat on the sofa in the parlor, a locale forbidden to people with food, and put our feet on the cocktail cable, a posture also forbidden. We were comfortably ensconced without fear of intrusion and parental restraint, counting on an afternoon of quiet, while our mother suffered her migraine in a darkened room above.

I had flicked through the book.

"The Pobble Who Has No Toes." I intoned. Toby screamed a laugh and immediately clamped his hands over his mouth, eyes cast to the ceiling.

"Shut up, Toby, if you want me to read."

"Shhhhhhh." he complied.

That evening while finishing my homework at the desk in my room, I noticed I had brought the book that I had read to Toby with me. I glanced at the spine and then riffled through the pages. I spread it open to the fly-leaf. There was an inscription:

To Arianna,

on the occasion of her tenth birthday many happy returns of the day.

From Elsie Chandor
November 9, 1901

The inscription was extravagantly flourished in purple ink that had faded on the yellowing page. Something stirred in my memory. The name was somehow familiar. The more I tried to remember, the more elusive the memory became. In frustration I decided to use my technique of thinking hard about something else completely different. Then the answer would come to me in a flash, like a teasing elf whisking ahead of the chase, but returning to captivity when he felt safe and forgotten. A few minutes of intense concentration burned away and I abandoned my quest. The book was latter put away on a shelf and my interest in its mysterious inscription disappeared into what Mother called the forgetting part of my mind. The nimble elf had gone. Although I occasionally took the book down to regale my brother with what he called "another silly poem" and brought it along with my personal treasures to Nammy's house much later, Arianna in her birthday dress and Elsie with her purple ink and quill pen had melted into the past.

Just before Easter, my Great-Grandfather died, and Uncle Cliff decided that the usual festive family gathering was out of the question. I wasn't allowed to go to the viewing or the funeral and had to depend on Ardath's and Cam's florid retelling of the particulars.

We stopped at Cliff House after church on Easter morning, bearing an Easter lily in a pot wrapped in green foil for Great-grandmother and a white hyacinth in a pot wrapped in pink foil for Great Aunt Evelyn. My aunts were there decorously dressed in black; my uncles stood around with their hands clasped behind their backs. Each had brought Great-grandmother an Easter lily in a pot wrapped in green foil and Great Aunt Evelyn a hyacinth in a pot wrapped in silver or pink foil. Aunt Shirley fanned her red-tipped fingers in front of her face looking pained and complaining that but for the cigar smoke, the place smelled like a funeral parlor. Aunt Jeanette sniffed and dabbed at her eyes with a handkerchief.

Michael ran up to me and pulled up his lip. "See? Yook. Youcung see new toos cungin in!" I had no desire to look at my cousin's drooling, gaping gums so I smiled smugly and patted him dismissively on the head.

"I got a nickel for it! A *nickel*" he bragged. Uncle Tim bent down, frowned his displeasure and shook his head despairingly at his avaricious child.

Ralph was in the sun room pawing through the Sunday funnies, making himself mercifully scarce. The adults circulated gravely, holding small glasses of wine and murmuring hushed platitudes. I went in search of Ardath and Cam, who had wisely left the sanctimonious post mortem and defected to the library where I finally found them crouched on the floor over a Parchesi board. They glanced up at me briefly and returned to their game.

"It's Josie. Nosy Josie." Cameron was examining the board. He swiveled and sat down facing me. "Nosy Josie, did you bring a posy for Matilda and Evelyn? Hmmmmmmm?"

Ardath barked scornfully at her brother. "Shut up, Cam. Don't be stupid. You always act so stupid. Sit down, Jo."

I did so, obediently.

"Well, you missed a really good funeral." Ardath began, sighing and casting her eyes heavenward, as if to catch a glimpse of her recently departed ancestor. She rolled over on her back and flung her arms wide. "A really, *really* good funeral, wasn't it Cameron? Too bad you couldn't have been there, Jo." She smiled pityingly and shrugged.

"There were hundreds of people, *important* people and scads and scads of flowers. "*Some* people came from far away. Far, *far* away." She swept her arm around gracefully. "Our grandfather was an important personage. A *very* important personage." She closed her eyes and folded her hands on her chest, smiling.

"Don't you ever shut up?" Cameron asked crossly. "It's time for you to shut up, Ard."

"People we hadn't seen in *years*." she continued, ignoring her rather. "People came from *everywhere*. People who ...."

Cam jumped up, startling me. "SHUT UP, Ardath. Leave it alone!"

But of course, she didn't leave it alone.

On the way home I simmered with resentment. I was almost as old as Ardath and Cameron, and they were allowed to go to the funeral, why wasn't I? I flung myself against the back seat of the car, determined to question my parents further about my banishment from this important event. It wasn't fair, it just wasn't fair.

As soon as we got back to our house, I confronted my mother.

"Nammy was at the funeral! Why didn't she come to see me?"

Mother started back, staring at me as though I had turned into a frog, or some other loathsome thing. Her face tightened.

"She wasn't there. Who told you that?"

"Never mind!" I was close to tears.

"Joanna," she began.

"Never MIND! You don't love me! You don't care about me! I hate you!" I turned away enraged, already feeling my righteous footing slipping beneath me, like a tilting fun-house floor. I stomped upstairs, nursing my rage against the selfish cruel family I was unfortunate enough to have been born into.

Excerpt from Jo's Journal—July 14th, 1940

My father came to see us yesterday and he had to leave this morning. He said he had to go to see mother and take care of some things. Everything is so secret. They never tell me anything. My father is very sad and serious. Not like Alonzo at all. Alonzo is fun. Nammy told me to make a card to send to Mother, so I asked, is she still sick? She didn't really answer but told me if I sent her a card, she would feel better. I didn't see how but it didn't matter, I had to do it anyway.

In the afternoon there was a storm with lots of thunder and lightening. I pretended not to be scared and Ardath pretended to be scared. Later we couldn't find Andrew for a long time and then we finally found him in the back of the pantry where the kittens had been born where he made a fort. Maybe he was hiding from the storm, or maybe he was hiding from us. Anyway, we were greatly relieved to find him. We will know where to look next time. I'm learning to talk to him, sort of a talk, because he can't hear. I signal things in Indian Sign Language (that's funny, because he is half-Indian) and he sort of answers me back with his own gestures. He is really very smart, if you just get to know him.

As the weather finally warmed into a tender late spring, I reminded my parents of their promise to take us back to the Fair once more before it closed. Mother did not want to go; she made it very obvious, with her deep sighs and pained glances at my father. My mother hated crowds and noise. I had noticed that she had become increasingly repelled by the proximity of anyone and everyone. She was extremely susceptible to loud sounds, holding her hands over her ears, squeezing her eyes tightly shut as though in pain.

I, however, remained stubborn and summoned all my merciless childish resources, playing on their sensitivity to broken pledges and idle children, lifting my voice to a strident, invidious whine. Being unscrupulous as well, I enlisted Toby in my campaign. He rose to the challenge like a seasoned warrior and inveighed against our oppressors in the most odious, fractious manner. I was proud of him. When all else failed I said we would go with Aunt Jeannette and Ralphie, or even Aunt Shirl and Mikey-the-monkey. My ace in the hole worked like a charm; mother grudgingly relented and they made tentative plans to go on a weekday after school let out in mid-June. I kept them to their promise, reminding them on a weekly basis that if we didn't go, we would never have such a wonderful experience again, it would be gone forever and the opportunity-of-a-lifetime would be lost to their children. Mother tried to ignore me and father just shook his head and laughed softly.

The day of the trip finally arrived, and as it turned out, we went with Aunt Shirley and Uncle Tim and Michael. We crowded into the station wagon and set off for Flushing Meadows and the Greatest Fair in the History of the World. I felt smug and elated that we were going; so many unfortunate children all over the world would never know its wonders.

From what we called the "way back" Toby hooked his chin over the back seat and squinted both his eyes at me smiling. (I had been trying to teach him to wink). He spoke in a comically lowered voice:

"We made it, Jobiska."

We laughed at our private joke and endure Michael's show-off antics for the hour's ride to the Fair.

Excerpt from Jo's Journal: August 20th, 1940

It has been raining for two days and I was just lying here thinking of the last time we went to The World's Fair. It seems so long ago now. So many people came to visit it from so many different places all over the world. It was very exciting!!! Just looking at the buildings, the waterfalls and fountains was like visiting a foreign country, right here in America! There were huge statues, some had no clothes on. Cameron had told me they were "ballzass naked" I didn't know what that meant but I didn't want him to think I was stupid so I didn't say anything. There was a show called the Aquacade where instead of dancing or skating, the ladies in sequined bathing suits swam together to music. What I liked best, though, I think, since Mother didn't let us on the Life Savers Parachute Jump, which I REALLY, REALLY wanted to go on more than anything else in the world, was Futurama, inside the Perisphere. It was so exciting being up so high, in this great big dome, seeing how everything was going to be so wonderful in the future, it made everybody very happy. But the best part was the way the Trylon and Perisphere sang. There was beautiful chiming music that filled the air and the sky and lovely blue lights revolving all around as we left the Fair. Mother didn't remember the music at all. She didn't remember much of the Fair. She might as well not have gone.

I have to go down to tea now. I'll tell you more when I come back.

Your faithful friend and companion,
Joanna

I had found it hard to comprehend that the beautiful, elegant, powerful entity that was the New York World's Fair would be reduced to rubble by the time I went back to school in the fall. Not only did it seem like a wasteful desecration of a magnificent work of art, but it didn't seem possible that this marvelous world *could* be destroyed. I asked Father why THEY would do such a terrible thing and he pondered briefly, I think, to try to form an honest response understandable to a ten-year-old, but also for an answer that satisfied himself as well.

"They're finished with it, Jo. It served its purpose. I guess they don't need it anymore." he finished lamely.

This answer was, of course, most unsatisfactory and I told him so at some length. He didn't listen, of course, and it was no use to ask mother, who didn't know or care.

"I should have run away to the parachute jump and jumped to my death like Icarus!" I shouted to my empty room.

"Who's Icarus?" Toby stood in the doorway, looking around warily to see who I was yelling at.

I rolled over on the bed and growled into my pillow. "Go away Tobiska. You wouldn't understand. Nobody understands. Nobody cares."

They were going to sack my golden city, as the Vandals and the Huns and the Visigoths did in the Dark Ages. There would be rapine and pillaging. I didn't really know what that meant, but I was sure it was terrible and the Vandals and Visigoths of New York and New Jersey would far outdo their savage predecessors of old Europe. The sky would darken, and powerful whirlwinds would rise and suck up all the houses. There would be plagues and hail and sleet and fire storms; the sea would come to a boil. The four horsemen of the Apocalypse: skeleton soldiers on skeleton horses would cut us down like chaff with their gleaming scythes dripping blood, and the screams of widows and orphans would be heard throughout the land. I felt like an orphan, weeping beside the waters of Babylon. "Go away Toby!" I had begun to cry.

"Jo-BIS-ka!" Toby hadn't left and was crooning to me from the doorway. My grief aborted and I bounded up to a sitting position.

"I SAID GO AWAY! I'm going to cry 'till I die!"

"Jo-BIS-ka!" this time with a giggle.

I threw myself back on the bed with a moan. "I can't stand it!"

Suddenly there was someone beside me.

"Open your eyes, Jobiska!"

I groaned and opened my eyes. Toby was looking down into my face very soberly.

"If you are very, *very* VERY good, you can come with us to Jones Beach next week. But only if you are very, *very*, VERY good." He was ticking verys off on his fingers with comic solemnity and I had to laugh. He joined me laughing loud and clear and I punched him with my pillow.

I would not die after all. Maybe *after* we went to Jones Beach. There was nothing I could do to save my golden city anyway. I would have to learn to live with the vision of the future it promised.

The summer was release, freedom and wanton happiness. Delivered from the pressures of arithmetic homework, messy, tedious geography projects, and smelly, bossy teachers who slammed the pointer on your desk for no reason. I was a prisoner escaped. This was *my* time. I would be wild and mindless until I was recaptured and returned to the dim dreaded dungeon of learning that smelled of pine soap and floor wax. I pushed that frightful thought away from me and wallowed in my freedom. My parents left me to my own devices and Toby, who was no longer a baby, had quickly learned to become unobtrusive, even devious, and found many new ways to amuse himself. If he needed help or comfort, he came more and more often to me. Our mother was in the background, fragile and reclusive. She reminded me of the plant that folds its leaves together and pulls away from you when you touch it. My father, who served as District Sales Manager for what was left of my Great-grandfather's company, was away a great deal, supervising the salesmen in his charge. Mother's routine was unremarkable. She could most often be found curled up on the chaise lounge in the parlor with a book. Sometimes she went shopping or visited a friend for tea. When Father returned from what he called "the mercantile wars", Mother seemed relieved and almost happy, sometimes ignoring us completely. This didn't bother me, and I don't think it bothered Toby much, either.

"Jobiska! What are you doing?" he would ask commandingly.

If my activity was something he could be included in, of we went together. If not, I'd tell him that he was much too puny and dumb and send him away with his soldiers or a coloring book. He'd whine and I'd whine back, but he accepted my authority and hardly ever gave me any grief.

The previous summer was the first time we visited Jones Beach. Toby had been stunned and frightened by sight off the incoming waves, so Father lifted him up kicking and wailing and walked slowly into the surf holding him close, pointing to something out to sea My little brother twisted against him, red faced and sobbing, reaching his hand back to Mother pleadingly.

"Go on, Toby! It won't hurt you! It's fun! Look!" Mother took my hand, and pulled me toward the surf. The water broke against our shins, sending a shining veil of water and a spattering of lacy loam onto the smooth brown sand. "Whee!" she crouched down awkwardly, splashing water on my Father's legs. Toby began a fresh spate of anguish, screaming so hard I thought he would hurt his throat.

"Oh stop it, Toby, you big baby!" I yelled at him. He stopped squalling, surprised, and looked down at me. I sat in the surf and stuck my tongue out at him. A wave crashed against me and I fell back into the sand. He hiccoughed and began to laugh. When my father tried to put him down, he began to cry again, so back he went to the big green umbrella and the tumbled beach towels far fromm the tumbling waves. I stayed on my back staring up at the sky, listening to the ocean, grumbling and threatening as it approached for another onslaught.

"After I die," I spoke silently to the sky with the wheeling birds and tattered filmy clouds. "I will come back as a seagull! I willI be free to go wherever I wish!" The wave burst over me, turning me, molding the sand beneath my body into lumps and hollows. I blinked and gasped. "And I will eat other people's sandwiches, and I will sit on the top of the sea and never sink!" A second wave hit me and spun me around, chuckling and hissing as it returned to the deep. Back under the umbrella Mother was wiping Toby's nose and giving him a graham cracker.

I remember that day so well; how short it had seemed, how I had to be dragged away at dusk with sand between my toes, in my hair and in my bathing suit. Toby had made a truce with the ocean and settled just beyond the the reach of the grasping waves where he built himself a sand castle, patting the sides carefully with his little red shovel. As we left, wrapped in our salty, sandy towels, Father stopped and turned us toward the pavilion. He stood straight, poking me between the shoulder blades, a signal to emulate him. From a loudspeaker somewhere inside the pavilion came the strains of the National Anthem, trumpeting metallically into the wind. A uniformed color guard stood at attention around the flag staff while the flag was lowered into the arms of one of its members. We, too, stood at attention while two of the guards ritually folded the flag into a little triangle. One of the guards tucked the flag under his arm. They then turned smartly and marched away.

Toby stood watching, mouth open, his pail and shovel clutched against his fat little belly. "Wow, Jobiska! Did you see that? Did you?" He turned and jumped up and down in front of me. "Do they put the water away, too? Jobiska? Do they?" I laughed and began to run toward the parking lot, as our parents trudged through the slipping, sloping sands, dragging armloads of beach paraphernalia. Toby ran, pleading for me to wait for him. Of course, I didn't.

More than a year passed before we visited the beach again. Toby skipped and hopped casually beside me, pretending not to be scared. He slowed down as we approached the surf and stopped. I watched as he stood, waiting as the advancing wave stumbled out of reach, unfurling a glittering sheet of water trimmed with yellow and white bubbles. As it reached Toby's toes, he began to giggle and jump up and down. "It's back, Jobiska! The water's back!"

The day stretched out languidly, like a golden beast, and the sun moved hot and white across a sky that was beginning to foam with clouds. Toby had lost his fear. We dashed into the surf and dug holes and trenches to make our own tiny lakes and rivers. We made a castle with turrets and moats, dungeons and keeps, even a tower for a captive princess. The sea moaned and sighed rhythmically and crept up to our marvelous creation. Toby howled and shoved himself on his bottom back from the wave which had slid up and bitten a moist chunk from the castle. I joined his howls and the furious ocean claimed our fragile art, sucking and crushing it in its hungry mouth.

It was the last summer before the world changed; sometime before the brazen fall flowers pushed aside the faded summer lilies. And Paris had fallen.

I was horrified by the unashamed display of sorrow in evidence at Cliff House, not being able to relate to Evelyn and Cora's halcyon girlhood days in the City of Light. I had a mental picture of the Eiffel Tower bending and falling into the fountains, crushing statues and stone lions and a flaming Arc de Triomphe crumbling into the Champs d'Elysees.

"Paris has fallen! Ah ma belle Paris! Ma pauvre belle Paris!"

I had never seen Great Aunt Evelyn cry, and it was an alarming sight. Cora, yes. She cried all the time. But Evelyn! Stalwart, staunch, steadfast Evelyn! I elected the better part of valor and sought out Ardath and Cameron. They had little patience to spare for the grieving women.

"REALLY! You'd think the world was coming to an end! Who cares what happens to the French! What a *gigantic* bore! Evelyn and Cora have been babbling in French ever since this stupid thing happened. I'm just so SICK of it!" Ardath was witheringly scornful.

"Maybe we should put out the Tricolor at half-staff! You know, have a funeral for the Froggies!" Cameron offered cheerfully, attempting to inject a little levity into the gloom laced outrage.

Ardath brightened considerably. "That's a GREAT idea, Cam. You know sometimes you are not as dumb as you look!" So, Cam, Toby and I began our search with Ardath at the lead, waving us on like Marianne at the barricades.

We burrowed and scouted from attic to cellar and were unable to locate the French flag that Great-aunt Evelyn had brought back with her from Paris. At the height of the search Toby and I were preemptorarily summoned and taken home before we had a chance to locate the sacred banner and observe the proper obsequies. I whined and begged to no avail; thus, I was in full sulk when we returned home for dinner.

"Not another silly poem, Tobiska!" I groaned.

"YES, YES, YES!"

"ONLY *ONE* TOBISKA!" I shouted, scowling fiercely.

'YES, YES, EEEE, YES." he jumped up, punching the air.

They went to sea in a sieve, they did;
In a sieve they went to sea:
In spite of all their friends could say,
On a winter's morn, on a stormy day
In a sieve they went to sea.
And when the sieve turned round and round,
And every one cried, "You'll all be drowned!"
They called aloud, "Our sieve ain't big;
But we don't care a button, we don't care a fig"
In a sieve we'll go to sea!"
Far and few, far and few,
Are the lands where the Jumblies live:
Their heads are green, and their hands are blue;
And they went to sea in a sieve.

We watched the sea gulp down our beautiful castle. Toby whimpered.

"Never mind, Tobiska. We'll build another one where the water won't get it, EVER." I said firmly.

There was a moment of unspoken sorrow as the wind blew hollow whisking sounds around us and the sea sucked back into the unknown. The gulls whistled and squealed and the sun slid behind a purple cloud. Our mother's voice calling us to lunch threaded through the buffeting wind and echoing surf.

Toby spoke.

"I guess it just can't be helped. It was such a nice castle, too. It just wasn't meant to be."

He gazed at the hollow where our castle had been; he seemed so wise and sad that I had to laugh and laugh.

END OF BOOK ONE

Book Two

".... with joy tempered with contempt ..."

"We're up here, we haven't a timetable, why don't you want to go to Edgecombe?"

On the spur of the moment John and I had decided to take a post-Labor Day vacation: no destination, no restrictions, no cares or worries. We had both needed to get away, to shake the weight of commitments and duties off for just a little while, and take a refresher course in self-indulgence. As one who had passed Family and Social Responsibilities and Obligations 101 with honors, I found it difficult to pull away from the relentlessly fallow territory of my origins.

As I packed and shut down the house, I gave myself the pep talk that I occasionally inflicted on others whom I regarded as in need of my counsel. Always chock-full of elevating aphorisms and cheery platitudes, my talks always made eminent good sense and I fully expected others to act upon my suggestions. Taking my own advice, however well thought out and sensible, was quite another thing.

We left just after dawn, as John was greedy to catch every possible moment of our rare mutual holiday. My mind flicked back to the house, as we moved further from my essential care of it. I inventoried pre-travel tasks such as turning off the gas under the kettle, shutting the windows, watering the plants, unplugging the iron. What else? There must be something else. I fretted quietly as we headed north.

John was relaxed and had easily slipped into his vacation mode, something I wish I could have done. I envied the ease with which he would fall asleep after a stressful day or escape to a ball game or book, seemingly untroubled by the pressures that attended his work.

I shook myself and the house faded from my thoughts. I knew not to speak of my worries; John would make light of them and make a sorry joke about the house being insured and that we could always live with his parents.

"I didn't say I didn't want to go to Edgecombe."

We drove a while in silence.

"I don't even know if it's still there."

More silence.

John had obviously given this some thought. "Well, we could maybe drive up that way, see if there's a place we could get some lunch."

It wasn't quite a question, but I was to reply to it as such.

I sat up straight. "Let's just get some lunch. OK?" I smiled and turned to look out the window.

Excerpt from Jo's Journal: September 1, 1941

I'm writing this on the train going back to New Jersey, or actually New York, where Uncle Clifford's driver will pick me up at Grand Central Station. Before she left Nammy's, Ardath told me that I was very fortunate to be admitted to St. Anne's, the new school I'll be going to. She said they weren't taking any more boarding students, but as a special favor to Uncle Clifford, they are going to let me in. She said it is a very scary school, and the nuns who are very holy women, will hit you with a ruler until you bleed if you misbehave, and make you eat a bar of soap if you don't learn the lesson. I don't think I'm going to like it there.

I just ate my sandwich and apple Nammy packed for my lunch.

Andrew came with Alonzo to see me off on the train. (Alonzo calls him "Little Sprout" after the grandson of Skywoman who made all the animals small.) Andrew is funny. He cried when I left.

I must sign off now, dear Journal.

Your faithful friend, Jo

There must be a special place in Hell for people like my dear cousin Ardath who delighted in the torment of others. I was so terrified of going to St. Anne's that it made me quite ill. Uncle Clifford and Aunt Evelyn were genuinely puzzled at my panic-induced diarrhea and sudden tempests of tears. Evelyn finally lost patience and confronted me the day before school was to begin. My bags were packed and I was freshly vetted for my new academic career. She sat on my bed where I lay sobbing dryly. She spoke sternly.

"Now, my girl. I think we've had about enough of this. Up you go, Come on!" She lifted me by the shoulders and gave me a little shake. "You know the doctor says there's nothing wrong with you. You've no temperature and you haven't a rash or anything else that really sick people have." She softened as I fell limply on her shoulder and cried quietly.

"Oh dear! There, there, Joanna. Stop. Stop now. I have something to tell you."

I flopped back on my pillow miserable and disheveled. Evelyn looked up and away, into her past.

"You know when I was just a few years older than you are now, I was to be sent to France to study one summer." She beamed, as though this made everything all right and crystal clear.

"I was so sick! There was nothing wrong with me, you understand, but I was *so* sick, I couldn't keep anything on my stomach. JUST LIKE YOU." she pointed at me meaningfully with each word.

"My mother was furious, of course. Father, well ..." she shrugged. She gazed away thoughtfully, then shook herself and turned to me.

"Do you know what they did?" I'm not sure she even saw me shake my head. She continued quickly.

"THEY MADE ME GO TO FRANCE! Where I had the best time I ever had in my life, EVER!" She paused momentarily.

"Now get up, Joanna, you are going to bathe and dress and I shall take you over to meet with Sister Joseph and afterwards we will have lunch and an ice cream at Rumplemeyers'. Come along now!" She rose imperially; there was no denying her command.

Of course, I got up from my bed, bathed and donned my new uniform with its ASA badge, stiff creases and itchy seams. We met with Sister Joseph and had lunch at Schrafft's in the City and had ice cream at Rumplemeyers'. I vowed that I would never incur the wrath of any of the nuns who held over me the threat of dire punishment of the most excruciating pain. I knew this must be true, Ardath wouldn't lie to me.

"Tell me about Edgecombe."

John brought me back to the present where I had to sort out the tangle of memories.

I shook myself and smiled.

"Edgecombe. It was my favorite place in the world. Nammy was a mother and more and I got to do things I never could have done at home; not just because there were more places and things to explore, but because my mind was free. I would get dirty, really, really, dirty! Nammy would pretend to be shocked when I came home from one of my adventures at the end of the day and she'd dump me into the big cast iron tub in the summer kitchen and threaten to scrub the skin off my back." I laughed happily at the memory.

"Sounds like a great place to spend the summer." John said.

"I wanted to live there, *always*. The house was so homelike. I'm not sure how to put it. Not just because it was cluttered and..." I groped for words. "And, I don't know, friendly? Nammy didn't fuss about things like how I sat at table, or folded my napkin, or things like that. I was comfortable. I felt like I was with people who cared about me and didn't resent me." I fell to musing again. We drove for a while in silence.

Mixed feelings of loyalty and a need to purge old hurts prevented me from sharing some of my memories with John. He would be indignant on my behalf. Which I knew would leave me in an unsettled state, unwilling to reexamine the past and its puzzle. So, I began an abridged summary of my intermittent stays at Edgecombe.

I had been trying to submerge the pain and anger I felt. My cheeks flamed and my heart beat so furiously I thought it would leap from my chest. I sought refuge in the workshop, away from the scene of my humiliation.

"Oh, what is it, little one?"

Alonzo had immediately seen through my guard and was so solicitous that I broke down and burst into tears. He patted me gently on the back. "Hey! What happened? What's the matter? It's that Cameron and Ardath, ain't it? Ah, don't you pay no never mind to those two. They think they piss sunshine, they do. Have mighty high opinions of themselves, they do, yeah."

The flood of tears had begun to subside. I rubbed my cheeks and nose with the back of my hand and snuffled loudly. Alonzo spoke soothingly.

"You know what to do with people like that, little one? This is what you do."

He bent forward from where he sat on the battered workbench and narrowed his eyes.

"This is an old Indian trick. Works every time." He leaned closer, narrowing his eyes until they were black slits. He began to hum, almost inaudibly, and nod. He gravely shook his head back and forth and raised his hand very slowly and pointed at me, then tapped his temple sentiently. Then he smiled and turned away, continuing to hum. I found myself imitating his motions, trying to follow with my eyes squinched up. "Good! Good! You just do that, they won't know what to make of it. Maybe even think you're crazy If they think they got you mad or sad, they're satisfied. If they think you don't care ..." he bent toward me, leering, " ... it'll drive *them* crazy!" He started to laugh his big laugh and I began to giggle.

I had wanted to tell him what had prompted my outrage, but Alonzo's compassion and lively pantomime had almost driven the hurt away.

"Aw, pay no attention to them, little one. They just jealous 'cause your gramma likes you best. Oh yes, she does! I know for a fact!" he nodded emphatically, laughing softly now.

I was comforted by that thought and hoped it was true. Indeed, l needed it to be true.

This was where I could go for solace: a ramshackle, jerry-rigged, messy asylum of consolation and confirmation. I settled down in a corner on a cushion of wood shavings and scraps, making myself small, wrapping my arms around my knees.

"What are you doing, Alonzo?"

"Doin' my boots. Have to give 'em a good rub with Neatsfoot Oil now and again to keep 'em supple. Keep the wet out, you know."

He was buffing his shoe with a dirty cloth, paying special care to the cracks and scuffs, the wounds of many years and miles of wear. I watched him closely for a minute. He rhythmically whipped the rag over the shoe, grunting and humming. Then he held the boot at arm's length and gazed at his handiwork appraisingly.

"What's Neatsfoot Oil, Alonzo?"

"What's Neatsfoot Oil?!" He shook his head, shocked at my ignorance. "Well, Neatsfoot Oil is the special grease I get for my boots to keep 'em from dryin' and breakin' up." he smiled.

He put down the shoe and turned, hands on knees, elbows out. He grinned his funny crooked grin.

"See, these guys go out and hunt down all the little Neats and cut off their feet, and squash 'em all up to a jelly and then they put it in this here bottle." He held it up for me to see.

I was fascinated. He continued, nodding seriously.

"Haven't you ever seen any of them Neats in the woods, runnin' around on their little stumps?" He got up quickly and thumped around the workshop, rocking stiff- legged and wide eyed, jabbing his cane in the air. "You're always in the woods, you must've seen some Neats! They just go stumpin' away!"

I had started to giggle. It was all he needed for encouragement and did a theatrical turn, hopping and dodging, accompanying his dance with anguished hoots and gargles.

I was laughing heartily now, clapping and waving my hands.

I glanced up quickly to see Nammy, who had paused at the door of the shed. She was headed for the garden to harvest a cabbage for dinner and held a kitchen knife in her hand.

"What are you doing to that child, 'Lonzo?"

Alonzo crouched down and whispered to me, casting a mock terrified look at Nammy. "Looka that. She's gonna go get some Neatsfeet! Gonna cut them all off with her big knife!" I flung myself on the floor, kicking my heels, screaming and howling with laughter.

Nammy walked away toward the garden, shaking her head. "You two are crazy." I heard her say as she departed.

"See? See?" Alonzo dragged me to my feet still helpless with laughter. "It works! Everybody thinks we're crazy!"

We filled our lungs with the wonderful purgative of laughter. Nothing can hurt if you could laugh like that.

Excerpt from Jo's Journal—September 20, 1941

Dearest, dearest Journal:

I don't like staying at St. Anne's. It is gloomy and old and I have to room with a boring little tattle-tale. Her name is Patricia Jane Cahill. I call her Janie for short. She doesn't like it, and I'm glad. She has been at St. Anne's for three years and she thinks she's so great. She calls the nuns by their given names behind their backs. It's "Dominic this and Ursula that." It makes me sick. The nuns are really not so bad, as long as you behave and ask the right questions. And give the right answers. There are only a few of us Protestants at that school and the Catholic girls look at us as though we have two heads. Janie told me that they pray every evening for our conversion, otherwise we will burn in hell. WELL!

One thing that makes me sad is that I can't keep my journal while I am at school. Please forgive me, Dear Journal. If I tried to write I know Janie the rat will tattle on me, then they would take you away from me and then I would really be in trouble. So, I have to wait until a weekend comes and I can go to Cliff House where I can pretty much do as I like, as long as I'm quiet and mind my P's and Q's.

I thought I was in trouble the first week at St. Anne's. I was called to Sister Joseph's office. (Sister Joseph is the Principal). She looked at me queerly and asked me if I was happy at St. Annes. I lied and said yes. I didn't think it would make any difference. I was scared anyway. She asked me if I had become good friends with Patricia Jane and I lied and said yes. She talked for a while and told me to come to her if I had any problems. I lied and said I would. I didn't know I was crying in my sleep. Or maybe Janie the snitch was lying. Can a Cathoclic lie to a nun? I don't know. I don't know who I can ask, either.

I must leave you for a little while, Dear Journal. I'm being called to supper.

Your Faithful Friend and Companion,
Jo

"Ardath, if you're a Catholic, could you ever, I mean, would you lie to a nun?"

Ardath rolled over on her back, still reading her book. She could always be found on the floor of the library, the sun room, her bedroom or where ever she found a solitary patch of carpet. She eschewed the furniture, even the ugly comfortable overstuffed chairs and couches. The floor was Ardath's place.

She lowered the book to her chest and regarded the ceiling for a moment.

"I think anybody can probably lie to anyone anywhere at any time." Then she turned and looked at me solemnly. "I think it's probably not a good idea, though. You could get in trouble. Besides, you're not Catholic. You've nothing to worry about." She resumed reading.

"No," I persisted "I mean another person, a Catholic, would she lie to a holy nun, an *important* holy nun. I mean without committing a venal sin and maybe burning in Hell?"

Ardath sighed deeply and closed her eyes. "You mean *venial* not venal. Besides what you *really* mean is MORTAL sin. That is much, much worse. For that you could burn for eternity in hell, along with us Protestants." She casually returned to her book.

My cousin was so smart. I slavishly hung on everything she said. She was a font of information trivial and forbidden and my source of truth. Anyone who could declaim as Ardath did with such imperious confidence, must be infallible.

On Sunday night I was driven back to St. Anne's by Great Aunt Evelyn, who kept up a constant stream of chatter, I think more to distract me than to impart any information. I ignored her gloomily and looked out of the window at the weeping skies and limp dripping trees. The weekend had gone so fast and the week ahead loomed interminably with its long dreary classes and the infuriating company of Saint Janie, my roommate, sighing sanctimoniously and clacking her Rosary. My eyes filled with tears of self-pity.

"Aunt Evelyn, why can't I go back to my old school, where I went before?" She paused a moment before answering.

"It would be too far to travel, since you're staying with us on holidays. St. Anne's is a very good school." I thought about this for a moment. She had not really answered my question, and too quickly retrieved the thread of her lilting chatter. I drooped back in the seat, resigned to my harsh sentence. For what I was being punished for, I couldn't imagine. I only knew that everything had changed.

Excerpt from Jo's Journal October 10, 1941

> *Dear, dear Journal:*
>
> *I have missed you so! Sometimes I think I will strangle Saint Janie she is such a pill. I wouldn't convert and spend eternity with all the angels and saints if it meant being in the same place as her. I would rather burn in hell! If I strangled her, I would burn in hell. But it would be worth it! I never thought I would miss my old school, but I do. At least I could go home at night and not be with HER. Why can't I go home? I know Mother is ill and in the hospital and Father can't take care of us because he has to work and visit Mother. I'm going to ask Aunt Cora. Maybe she'll tell me when I can go home.*
>
> *More later, dear Journal. I have to put out the light now or they will be in to yell at me.*
>
> *Yrs, Joanna*

In primordial times October signaled the close of the year. This was the death, both real and symbolic, of life and labor, when the ancients buried their year king and resurrected the dead.

The transition from the heat of summer to the cold, sleeping time of year is grandly adorned with celebratory colors, exalting the annual tribute to fruition and abundance. Here is a last voluptuous dance before winter's implacable invasion, with its chill long nights and bleak short days. October: the month of antic surprises. One might wake to fling off the oppressive comforter on an Indian summer morning so mild that the bird will postpone its journey and the bare limbs of quiescent plants quicken and burst with sharp green life. Or one could rise from a chilled bed to close the window only to find a day of crisp silver frost and clean cidery air, jolting the body to wakefulness and delight.

As we drove north, I relaxed, attempting to relieve my subdued senses of their habitual restraints. I felt bathed in the vivid hues around us, the air prenaturally light with reflected color, laughing with wind and the percussive rush and lash of leaves wallowing in a happy bacchanalia before being cast away forever to a resonant regenerative earth.

I sat up straight. "John, let's stop a minute. Oh, anyplace. I want to look at the mountains."

He slowed the car and pulled into a lay-by that bulged away from the curving road and offered a panorama of arching gold and crimson mountains that climbed away into a tenebrous distant silence. We got out of the car wordlessly and walked to the edge, grey-toothed with boulders of rough granite that skirted the tilt where our mountain fell away into brushy, whispering shadows.

"God, that's gorgeous!" He turned to me, smiling. "You feeling any better?"

I was unaccountably annoyed with his question and decided not to respond.

"Have you ever felt that you could fly? I mean launch yourself into the air, not like a bird, but like jumping into the wind and being held up by the air?' He looked puzzled, so I went on quickly. "Did I ever tell you about Sky Woman? How the geese brought her down from heaven to earth? She was the Grandmother. Her daughter gave birth to twin boys who created all things: animals, rivers, trees that dripped sugar, mosquitoes that cut down trees!" I was astonished at how vividly I remembered the story and it made me laugh. John was looking at me oddly.

"Oh. don't pay any attention to me! I'm just a little crazy, that's all! Ask anyone!" I kept laughing and returned to the car, John following behind me. I turned suddenly and snapped at him. "I feel fine!"

I immediately regretted my show of temper and quickly hugged him, all the while avoiding looking into his face. I mumbled a childish apology. It wasn't good enough,

"Do you know anyplace we can get something to eat?" His voice was detached and almost impersonal; he had brushed aside our little clash as though as it had never happened. (What we can avoid, we can forget. Oh yes, that's right: it's really very simple.)

I made an effort to match his tone. "I think there may be something around Catskill. It's changed so much, though. We'll just have to try our luck. John, I'm sorry,"

He reached over and took my hand. His face was expressionless as he stared at the road ahead.

Excerpt from Jo's Journal—October 25, 1941.

Dear Journal:

I am going to confide in you and only you, so no one will ever, ever know about this. I thought about who I could talk to and I can't think of anyone at all so you, as my closest confidante must listen. Please understand, dearest friend I need to talk to someone.

I think I'm going crazy. I feel so strange and think such terrible things that I get really scared. No, not things like killing Jane the Pain. Anybody would want to do that except for maybe Sister Joseph or Sister Imelda the religion teacher, who is such a stick. But things I'm not supposed to think about, like people's bodies and doing bad things to each other and touching people under their clothes. Sometimes I feel so strange and hot I get sick to my stomach and I want to scream. I try not to think about forbidden things and I end up thinking about them all the time, even in arithmetic and at chapel when we are supposed to think about God. This must be a terrible sin, Dear Journal. Why am I so bad? I don't want to be. I can't even look at Ardath and Cam in the face when I have these bad thoughts.

I am going to try very, very hard to be good. I am going to put a stone in my shoe and a pin inside my undershirt so it sticks and scratches me. This is called mortification, and some people become saints doing it. I bet they never thought about their cousins naked in the bath together.

Next week, Dear Journal.

Your friend in mortification, Joanna

"Do you know what I did when I was a kid? I put stones in my shoes so I would stop having salacious fantasies about my cousins. Isn't that a riot?"

John and I had found a nearly empty little restaurant in New Paltz and were sharing a carafe of wine and some sort of vegetarian sandwiches on flat bread. A solitary late-summer fly was swinging lazily around the room, occasionally making an elliptical loop to visit us and inspect our food. Our waiter, a bored young man in need of a haircut and a nap slouched against the service bar and glanced with casual resentment around the room. He rested a surly look on us and sighed deeply.

John leaned toward me and smiled lecherously. "How fortunate that you have overcome your inhibitions, my dear! Heh heh heh!" He swirled the wine in his glass and coked an eyebrow. "Your cousins were undoubtedly sexually precocious and would have liked to recruit you in their exploratory games." He paused as though thinking about further comment then seemed to change his mind. He finally shrugged and added "It's remarkable that you came out as strong as you did from that unhappy bunch." Sometimes John didn't know when to drop the subject so I interjected lightly.

"Enough of my crazy cousins and my sexual awakening. Stones in my shoes and pins in my shift probably didn't do me any harm, but what a dumb idea. I probably got it from Saint Jane my pious roomie. What a bitch." I poked at the remains of my sandwich and watched the fly settle on a bit of limp lettuce doused in a pool of something gray and viscous that had been represented as the house french.

"They weren't all unhappy, all the time." I lowered my head and began to laugh softly. Something was slipping out from the forgetting part of my mind into the light of autumn.

"Do you know you have a dimple in your right temple, right there? When you laugh?"

He had interrupted my train of thought and I decided to take an initiative. "Of course, a dimple is when you laugh, you know, just like a lap is only when you sit and a fist is only when you need to smack somebody in the ear!" I rose from my seat in mock anger and punched him on the shoulder. John laughed and ducked and our waiter looked at us with mild interest. He sauntered over to our table where we drained our wine glasses and giggled, kicking each other under the table.

"You folks want anything else?" He reached for the order pad stuck in the back of his belt. He sniffed.

I looked up. "Have you any Calico Pie?" I asked soberly.

John turned his head to hide a smile.

The young tyro stared glassily at me with a look that said plainly: "Go away, lady." He sighed and rubbed the side of his nose. "We have apple pie, cherry pie," he consulted the back of his pad surreptitiously and John took pity on him.

"Just a check, please."

John paid the grateful young man who angled back to the bar urging us to have a nice day and to come back again real soon.

We left the little lunchroom rejuvenated and happy, sweetened by the golden day, our intimacy rekindled. A feeling of childlike abandon seized and held us. Later that evening we would make love fiercely and I would forget for a precious fragment of time the sorrow that still clung to me like a wretched implacable wraith.

Further along the ridge we stopped at an orchard to pick some end-of-season apples. The old farmer who sat in a bent folding chair under a faded beach umbrella could have been our waiter's Father. They both had the same shaggy hair, indifferent response and watery gray eyes. Challenged by his dour mien we lavished praise on his orchard, the beautifully pruned trees, the wonderful apples, his clever hand-lettered sign saying "U Pick 'em', and even his marvelous vista of the Catskills hunched up against the western horizon. Our curmudgeon, who never budged from his chair, seemed to soften and reddened visibly when John pressed an extra dollar in his hand. As we left, he raised his voice to thank us and direct us to " ... have a nice day," and yes: ..."you all come back again, real soon."

The afternoon seemed to have been caught up by the unremitting autumnal winds, rushing away from me with a dash of falling leaves and fading light. I became like a child, reaching out to grab the day, to make it wait, to last. It had been a transitory, fragile idyll when time seemed to accelerate with each moment of longing.

John and I wandered north through the venerable hills that had been settled time out of mind by farmers and burghers, teeming with energy and ambition. It was a region eventually abrogated by the flight of the young to aspirations beyond the compass of the hills and snubbed by industries burgeoning beyond the capacity of its intimate creases and corners. We eventually stumbled on a crumbling river town that clung to a beetling bluff above the Hudson where we found an ancient pub that offered food and drink to weary travelers and disillusioned locals alike. The fare was good, featuring gargantuan sandwiches and frosty mugs of draft beer. John picked at the shards of potato chips left on his plate. slowly and sleepily.

"I know you are curious about Edgecombe. I don't mean to be secretive, or possessive, or, I don't know. It's just that I have so many memories that remind me of things I want to put behind me. It wasn't that long ago; it just seems long ago."

John looked up and drained his beer. "It's O.K. Maybe some other time."

I felt as though he were being dismissive, and perhaps he was. I tried to put myself in his place. Was I being too self-absorbed? He had a life, too, and had had one Before Joanna. The beer and the turkey club much-to-big-to-finish, had brought me to a mellow drowsy state.

He spoke quietly and I was jolted into rigid wakefulness.

"Tell me about Toby."

I stared at him for a moment. John was the most attractive man I had ever met; not handsome, thank God. He was strong and smart, and he could make me laugh when there wasn't anything funny left in the whole world. I thought for a moment he would withdraw his request, fuss over my feelings, as he had so often done in past. But he didn't. He sat opposite me, chin in hand, waiting. A waiter in a dirty apron approached our booth and John motioned for refills; my signal to speak.

I looked over his shoulder past the fumed sticky partition into the past.

"Toby was the cutest, smartest little kid. You would have loved him. He was funny and very loving." I stopped, surprised at how dispassionate I sounded. I leaned forward and looked at my companion in the eyes. "He called me 'Jobiska' after the Pobble's Aunt. So, I called him 'Tobiska'. It was part of our secret, private language." I sat back and looked away. The tears had begun, silently and quickly.

There was a plangent moment as we breathed and waited, as one waits for a quiet summons. Still watching me, John reached in his pocket and brought out an only slightly-used handkerchief which he flourished and held out to me.

"Do you know what?"

"What." I blew my nose loudly. It was not a question. Did I really want to know?

"I think," he continued deliberately. ". . . that you are a most remarkable woman, besides being beautiful and entertaining. And I intend to take you to the nearest sleazy motel and make love to you without stopping until the bed collapses or the neighbors complain, whichever comes first." He concluded his extravagant proposal without expression and paused only when I began to laugh through my undamable tears.

"Oh, John! Whatever will I do with you? You are a hopeless degenerate! You must promise never, never to change!"

He began to laugh, the relief in his eyes so terribly endearing that I grew greedy for that sleazy motel with its fragile furniture and cranky inmates.

We did, indeed, find shelter that night in the rather seedy caravansary intuitively conjured by my randy mate, The Rainbows

End Motel, whose bug-incrusted sign grudgingly admitted to a vacancy. Relieved and grateful for a bed, *any* bed, we pulled the yellowed shades and fell on the protesting springs and lumpy, musty mattress laughing and loving.

At Cliff House we always happily turned out for one final bacchanalian wallow before the end of autumn.

The trees had shaken away their lovely leaves and stood quivering and naked. The world and sky looked vast and open, so much more expansive than it did with its lush embellishment of green. The wind ran free, lifting the light and scouring the earth, making it ready for its blanketed sleep.

Ardath, Cameron and I raked the Fallen leaves into chest-high fortresses, molding wells in the crimson-gold mountains so we could hide and burrow and have ferocious leaf fights. We screamed and plunged into our springy, particolored bed until we had to lay back exhausted, chests heaving, cheeks flaming, to watch the impossibly blue arc of sky above us. I closed my eyes and listened to the pop and hiss of my feathery bed as it settled beneath me and filled my lungs with the crisp piquant smell of dying leaves and pungent spice of a remote wood fire.

"Good grief!" Aunt Evelyn's voice sounded out across the lawn. "You children worked so hard to rake all those leaves and then you throw them all back where they came from!" She turned away smiling and shaking her head, knowing that we would eventually have to rake the leaves all up again if we were to have the bonfire so essential to the season's close.

We lay still, renewing our energies and spirits, loathe to return to the house with its required civilized deportment. I watched as a flock of starlings was caught in the net of the wind and dumped chattering and whistling into the quivering arms of an old elm. A few errant leaves drifted slowly down to settle on the earth, quilted now with the crimson and gold of autumn's arms. I suddenly wanted it to be winter, spring, summer, when I could put time and distance between me and this year; to be away, grown and strong, memories dulled and shorn of the bristles and spines that caused such pain. Time passes so slowly when one is sad and afraid.

Ardath and Cameron had been talking quietly in the depths of their leaf pile. Suddenly Cameron laughed and shoved his sister down in the leaves and jumped on top of her. Ardath screamed and flailed her arms, punching his chest and face. I got up slowly, shaking leaves from my clothes and hair, and started back to the house feeling bleak and alone. Walking around to where the back of Cliff House bordered the cliff I could see the Manhattan skyline stretching before me. I looked downtown where the thickened mist softened and distanced the towering buildings that poked up like jagged teeth at tip of the island's jaw. Directly across the river and to my left crouched the sloping smutty buildings of Washington Heights where the George Washington Bridge caught the edge of the city, arched over the Hudson and plunged into the palisades, wedding sleepy provincial New Jersey to the irrepressible lusty city. The air thrummed and a pulse beat in my head. Over the tight buildings and past the bridge's towers, if I stood on my toes, I could see Flushing Meadows, where the Trylon and Perisphere still stood for me, like tiny geometric toys amid the crumble of what was my city of the future. The future was gone; was I ever there?

I hitched myself up onto the low wall and glanced over at the bridge and shivered. When they were building the east tower, a scaffold slipped and all the men who were standing on it fell into the base, to be buried by a deluge of concrete as it roared into the foundation. They are all still there, in their overalls and work boots, eyes and mouths closed with stone, never to change, never to be eaten by worms or turned to dust. "Do you think ..." Cameron had mused after telling me this grim tale…: that future archaeologists, digging up the ruined city will come on the bodies and think: Ah! When they built the bridge, they made a sacrifice to the God of the River!' Yes! So, they will!" I stared at the base of the tower, as if by the intensity of my gaze I would be able to see the men molded in stone, hidden statues in the poses of dancers, arms and legs bent, reaching, jumping. Did they know what was happening? Did they have time to be scared? Or think of death?

"DON'T DO IT! DON'T JUMP!"

Ardath and Cameron surged up behind me and jerked me off my perch on the wall, inspiring an explosion of indignant rage and a few choice forbidden words. This, of course, delighted my cousins and after restraining my thrashing arms and kicking feet, kissed me soundly on each cheek and dumped me back into the leaves.

Their lilting voices faded as they ran to the house. "Shall we tell Evelyn that Joanna said 'Sonofabitch'? Goddamn right, we, will!" A chime of laughter rang along the wind and I laughed too, before I started to cry.

"Wake up, Joanna! Wake up! It's all right. It's all right." The, voice was distant and filtered through a void drumming with thunder and raging surf, pulling me into a harsh semi-consciousness full of shadows and unforgiving sorrow.

"You don't know, you can never know. It's not all right. It will never be all right."

The dream had returned with its fearful augury of something just out of the reach of my mind, needing to know and fearing it, terribly. I was running up a path that dropped away on both sides into some sort of abyss from which rose the sounds of crying and the crashing of waves. The road rose and widened. I could feel the spray of the surf and a gabble of voices that drowned out the crying. I hurried, my breath cutting my chest, my throat dry and cracking with cries I couldn't utter. Before me loomed a castle that had fallen to ruin, towers with ravens and bats, torn strings of ivy hung from broken walls, wafting and beckoning. The windows in the ruin were black and broken, all but one, and someone looked out at me from a room brightly lit and full of echoing laughter and faint music. I was afraid to look but was compelled to in the imperative of the dream state. Toby looked down at me and smiled. Oh Toby! He didn't move but he called out to me. "Jobiska! Come on up! There is a party here! Come on up!" He began to laugh happily and the pain in my chest burst. I turned and tried to run and the path had been covered by waves crashing and swarming towards me like the thick flow of death. I couldn't move and the waves engulfed me and stuffed my chest with terror.

"Joanna! IT'S ALL RIGHT! Oh my dear, it's all right!"

The dream melted away and the voice grew louder. I tried to open my eyes, and focused at last on Nammy, who was holding me tight, talking me away from the terror of my sleep.

"There, there, my dear. It's all right. You were just having a bad dream." My face felt hot and my throat hurt; I sobbed and moaned; I thought I would never be able to stop. Nammy continued rocking me, murmuring a soothing litany that didn't seem to stop the fear and pain. The room came into focus. Alonzo stood by the door looking alarmed. Beside him Andy had crept, silently curious. He was quickly shooed away by a look from Nammy and a gesture from Alonzo. I could hear voices in the hall. Clarity shook out the specters and I felt myself quieting.

"Is she all right? What happened?" Another murmur and gesture telegraphed from Nammy to Alonzo and the voices trailed away down the hall.

"It was just a dream."

Just a dream.

I struggled to emerge from the crushing nightmare I needed to believe the assurances of this person trusted above all others; the one who had never lied to me, who believed what I said, who *listened* to me. Just a dream, a dream that came back when you thought everything was going to be all right, a dream that left me in a trough of sorrow.

"Nammy ..." I began faintly.

"Shhhh!" she gently commanded, shaking her head and holding me closer. "You just get back to sleep. We'll talk in the morning. Joanna, it's OK."

I had begun to cry again. I had to cry: it hurt too much to try to stop.

Nammy stood up and looked down at me, shaking her head sadly.

"Poor baby." She paused. "Joanna, I'll stay with you, just sit over here, 'till you go back to sleep. OK?" She smiled and nodded. I nodded submissively, still sobbing dryly. If she would stay, I would be safe; I mustn't go back to that frightening dream. I lay in the dark staring at the ceiling, willing myself to wakefulness, waiting for dawn, when I knew all my demons would be banished by tie' light of a new day. Nammy began to hum tunelessly as she rocked in the chair just beyond the corner of my vision. She hummed and the chair creaked, and I fell into a soundless, visionless, merciful sleep.

The next morning Ardath and Cameron were uncharacteristically sober and solicitous. They peered at me over their breakfasts as though I had just emerged from a prolonged: illness or some sort of coma. Nammy darted quick warning glances at them as she moved between the stove and table. She was painfully cheery and I longed for her customary distracted bustle and funny asides, seemingly oblivious to my cousins' teasing and badgering, Ardath leaned toward me and cleared her throat. Nammy shot her a reproving look.

"How are you feeling this morning, Joanna?" my cousin inquired almost gently. Cameron frowned his concern and nodded, a little bit like a clown just popped out of a box.

I decided that I was at last in command of a situation, however trivial, and decided to take advantage of it. I had woken early with a surprisingly clear head and a gigantic appetite. I sighed and closed my eyes languidly and began to nod. I continued to nod for a moment, then opened my eyes. They were watching me gravely, nodding in unison, waiting for my brave response. I had to suppress a laugh.

"I feel ... much ... better. Thank you. It is good of you to ask." I sat back in the chair and half closed my eyes. I sighed deeply, watching them through the web of my eyelashes as they exchanged frowning glances. They looked back at me, genuinely bewildered.

"I think I'll go to my room and rest a bit. Thank you all so much for your concern." I rose regally and turned away so they couldn't see my emerging smile. I glanced out of the corner of my eye and caught Nammy, hand on hip, leaning against the stove, a knowing smirk on her face, which I noticed she shielded from her niece and nephew. She straightened and turned toward the stove grinning.

"That's a good girl, Joanna. You go on up and rest, we'll check on you later, maybe bring some nourishment, maybe a really runny egg ..." she was pursuing me into the hall as I ran upstairs choking back the giggles ..."or a lovely bowl of warm, soggy milk-toast ... mmmmm! Won't that be scrumptious?"

My cousins were beginning to rumble and Nammy returned to the kitchen laughing. "Come on, come on! It'll be lunchtime at the rate you two are going. Eat up!"

"Nammy ?" Ardath began inquiringly.

But Nammy had turned back toward the stove, singing loudly and off-key about Bill Bailey and a fine-tooth comb.

Their inquiries as to the state of my health, mental and otherwise, would have to wait.

Excerpt from Jo's Journal, November 26, 1941

Dear Faithful Friend:

We have been dismissed early for the Thanksgiving holiday and I am very relieved! I don't think I could stand another minute with Saint Jane the Pain. Ever since she found a mouse in her bed on Halloween and blamed it on me, she has been acting like a martyr and fumbling her beads loudly at night so I have trouble sleeping. I wish I could tell Sister Joseph that she is keeping me awake, but she would think it was just wonderful that my "little friend" (HAH!) was praying for me. She threw such a fit when she found the mouse, I thought she would have a seizure. Her face got red and she screamed, and spit all over the place. What a specticle! (sp?) I tried to stay out of the way and pretend to be sorry when all the Catholics were going to the Confession before evening prayers. When Janie came out from behind the curtain in the confessional box (it looks like a coffin. Ugh!) she looked over at me with a saintly look and kneeled down to say whatever prayers the priest gave her to make up for her terrible sins. She could kneel there forever, as far as I'm concerned. God can forgive her if He wants. I won't if I live to be a hundred years old.

Tomorrow is Thanksgiving and I am trying to feel good about seeing everybody. I will get up early and maybe help Edith set the table or something. Sort of stay out of the way, you understand. Somebody, I don't know if it was Nammy or Evelyn, or both, talked to Ardath and Cameron about me, I think. They are being nicer to me now. I don't know if I like this, I feel so strange and uncomfortable. Like I'm one of those freaks at the Fair, or something.

Well, I have to think of something to be thankful for and say a prayer about it. Sister Imelda said I should pray for all my family and friends, especially those estranged (sp?) from the true church. Whatever that means. They (the Catholics, that is) pray for the dead, too. This keeps them very busy, with all the people they have to pray for. I will stop now and say some prayers, especially for Nammy, Alonzo, and Andrew, my Mother, of course, who is still in the hospital, Father, the starving people in Asia and our President. I hope Great-grandfather isn't anywhere near God when he gets that last prayer.

Oh, and Toby.

Must close, Dear Friend, it's time for lights out. Good night, sleep tight, and don't let the bedbugs bite!

Yours with many Thanks, Jo

P.S. I did put the mouse in Janie's bed! And I'm glad! This is another secret you must swear on the Holy Bible you will never tell! I know you won't tell! You are a Dear and Faithful Friend.

I must go now and say my Thanksgiving Prayers.

Bye!

Thanksgiving that year was blustery and changeable. The sun, striving to brighten the day, was dimmed by sudden recurrent gusts, as though the wind were trying to blow out the light and return us to darkness. I tried not to think about the last time we all sat at this table; tried not to torment myself by looking for people who would not be there: Great-grandfather, Mother, Toby. But most of all I dreaded seeing my aunts and cousins again, all of us pretending that everything was the same.

Last year seemed like an old dream. Even Nammy's caring and constant attendance over the summer couldn't take away the odd numb feeling that the air had thickened around me so I had trouble walking and even breathing. Things had stopped, or paused at emptiness, and I had to make myself wake, when all I wanted to do was sleep. I had foolishly thought that Nammy would be with us at Thanksgiving because of that past summer's sadness and Great-grandfather gone, but of course she wasn't.

When Father arrived at Cliff House I answered the door and waited a clumsy moment before he hugged me and forced a smile.

"How's my Jo? You look good, real good! School OK?" He gave my braids a playful tug and turned away, rubbing his hands, nodding and smiling at Cora's offer of a highball. I don't think he was waiting for a school report or anything else I might ask or offer. I suddenly felt very sorry for him, and mercifully relieved of the burden of his expectations.

Aunts, uncles and cousins arrived in clumps that shifted from the foyer to the living room where respects and stilted greetings were exchanged. The personalities of the little family groups were almost comical in their presentations. The Aunt Jeanette troop paused smiling brightly, tilting and turning heads like birds at a feeder. Ralph with his hair slicked back stiffly did a hopscotch turn on the checkered tiles in the foyer and was immediately stilled by an admonishing hand each from his parents, who didn't even look at him or frown, but continued smiling brightly, nodding and blinking.

The Aunt Shirley troop advanced with spurious dignity into the living room where they imparted tender impersonal kisses on the female cheeks and smiles and perfunctory nods to the males. Michael was dressed impeccably and looked quite forlorn, despite his beamish grin. I felt myself shrinking as Aunt Shirley descended upon me.

"Oh, my dear, how are you? We pray for you every day. Don't we, Michael? Isn't that right, Timothy?" She pressed my upper arms in an ersatz hug and I felt less than comforted.

A falsely hearty rumble from Uncle Clifford offered drinks all around and he hurried away to the sideboard while Aunt Evelyn with her usual charm and alacrity moved through the chilly little group bringing warmth and some very small talk. Cora sat on the love seat discoursing earnestly with Great-grandmother, who nodded now and again with great distance in her eyes.

Alarming to admit, I found the company of my cousins some comfort and sought them out in the sun room where Ralph was holding forth on some of the more arcane fine points of etiquette.

"If you burp, you have to say 'excuse me', if you fart, you say '*pardon* me.'"

"That is one of the *dumbest* things, or maybe *the* dumbest thing I ever heard." jeered Cameron dismissively. "You are not *supposed* to burp or fart in front of anybody you have to apologize to, you twerp."

"Oh yeah? Well, that's how much *you* know!" Ralph responded indignantly.

"What's a fart?" Michael asked blandly.

Ardath, who had been lying on the rug reading a book seemingly oblivious to the boys' exchange, groaned, rolled her eyes and tented the book on the top of her head. "Really you all are the most *puerile* people I ever saw! Who cares what you do when you flatulate? REally!"

"She said I smell. I don't smell. Do I?" Michael plaintively asked the twin brother of the all-knowing Ardath.

Ardath had resumed reading her book, which was covered with something that looked as though it had once been a paper bag. "Joanna's here. Maybe you had all better shut up." My cousins turned to look at me curiously.

Michael ran up to me and asked "*I* don't smell, do I, Joanna? I took a bath, Mother made me take a bath before we came!" The last was said with such virtuous indignation that I had to laugh.

"You don't smell at all, Mikey. You're just fine." He smiled his relief and turned to Ardath. "See? Joanna says I don't smell!"

Ralph flopped himself dramatically on the chaise and brayed. "If you don't smell, why did God give you a nose, you dummy?"

Michael started to whinge and Cameron laughed derisively. "God, where did I get such dumb relatives? Where? I *ask* you!" Ralph was hooting and Michael continued to whine. Ardath flung her book away.

"Oh GOD!" she cried as though in pain.

Great Aunt Evelyn appeared at the door and summoned us to the table. I waited until my cousins got up, dusted themselves off and straggled out before I turned and went slowly toward the gathered guests. Cameron was waiting at the door and turned to me, feigning impatience. "Come on, Josie, you know we can't start without you!" I sketched him a brave smile and he stuck out his tongue at me.

We took our places at the table and waited for grace to be said. I studiously looked at no-one. Uncle Clifford cleared his throat ostentatiously, offered Uncle Timothy congratulations at his recent ordination as a Minister of the Gospel (of what denomination I never did know) and announced that to him would fall the honor of delivering Grace. The members at table crepetated into comfortable postures, coughed discretely, bowed their heads and fell silent.

I have often wondered why people, clustered by choice or custom, feel compelled to keep up a constant stream of talk, no matter how banal; filling the air with noise, nattering responses at cross purposes and as a shield to real discourse. For this reason, I have, since a very early age, engaged in what I call Creative Daydreaming. It is what I immediately fell into the moment Uncle Timothy droned "Let us Pray."

Like a bird I soared over a high white cliff overlooking the seashore. Below me scurried sandpipers on their stick legs, poking their beaks into the sand, and gulls white and brown that squeaked and screamed as they flapped and flailed the air and surf. No people were there; the ocean sounded like music. No umbrellas, no pavilions or rusting trash drums punched into the dunes. No little children, no evidence of civilization and its disruptions. The top of a dune cupped to windward, where poverty grass and beach plum clung and pulled away from the breeze. A little boat sat on the sand against a rock. Someone was sitting in it rocking it side to side like a cradle. I dropped down out of the sky and settled on an oarlock. I cocked my head. "Jobiska, you look just like a bird." "I am a bird." "I'm a fish. Like the Jumblies." "Like a porpoise", the bird corrected. "You don't look like a fish, you look like a Tobiska." the fish laughed and rocked his boat harder. "I am waiting for my sieve so I can go back to sea!" I lifted up from the boat with a surge of my feathered shoulders. "Don't go back, Tobiska! Stay with me!" The fish stopped rocking and looked up at me soberly "Oh but I must go back! I know now that the Seeze Pyder is gone." He leaned forward and up on his tail fins. "You know, I think it was never there. I think it was just make-believe." He nodded again and smiled "Oh Tobiska!" The fish laughed "Oh JOBISKA!" he bubbled and flipped into the sea. A breaker rushed toward me as I hovered waving a wing, he turned over and over again on his back and waved a fin. JoBISKa! If you're really, REALLY good, you will . . .." His words were swallowed by the sea. Something had seized me by the wing as I rose and I shuddered and tried to pull away.

"Joanna!" a low urgent voice hissed in my ear. I was staring at the basilisk mask of my Aunt Shirley. Her lips were moving but I didn't hear her words.

"We're having enough trouble trying to forget. Do you have to bring it up again? Now of all times?" Aunt Jeanette was speaking in a quivering voice.

Cora's hand on my arm relaxed its grip and I heard her start to snuffle. Shirley's head snapped toward her sister.

"We can only get over this with the help of Our Lord and Savior, Jesus Christ. We must not be afraid to ask His Grace and Blessings!" she intoned righteously.

"Clifford, I'm sorry, I didn't mean to open old woulds."

"No Timothy!" his wife interrupted. "We are trying to help in the best way we know how. Ted knows how much we care about you all! And Eleanor needs our prayers now more than ever."

Evelyn rose and took command, attempting to sweep together the scattered bits of good will that had evidently been shattered during The Reverend Timothy's Grace and my merciful daydream. She looked pale and strained. "Clifford, you can start to carve. Don't forget Mother Ashburn's portion. Edith! You can bring in the side dishes now! Thank you, Timothy. I'm sorry for the misunderstanding. Well, I think we can all dig in now! Bon Appetit!" She ended her cheery address breathlessly with a flap of her hands.

Cora continued to snuffle and to the left of me my father's hands remained still beside his plate.

I had a fleeting moment of regret for having missed the Grace that wreaked havoc on the family, but only briefly. My father's rigid face told me that the wound newly opened affected him most poignantly.

Serving dishes circulated in a silence punctuated occasionally by the clack of silver on china and a muffled "thank you". The atmosphere was considerably dampened.

"Someday you *must* give me the recipe for Edith's chestnut dressing. It is just *delicious*."

"You can't believe everything you hear on the radio or read in the papers, it just couldn't be as bad as they say it is."

"We don't go to the movies anymore. They have nothing but shootings and killings and sex. There's no wholesome entertainment anymore.

"Believe me, they got us into the last one, they'll get us into this one, too!"

"Any more stuffing?"

"Amos and Andy, or Vic and Sadc. One of those two. Funny, really funny!"

"Clifford, a little more white meat. Just a little, please."

"I don't know why Thanksgiving is on a Thursday, Michael. That's just the way it is."

"I don't want any creamed onions."

"The whole of Europe will be in Hitler's clutches within a year, you'll see. The English can't stop him. The Nazis are too strong. Too strong. They've got the Krupps machine behind them. The British, nothing, nothing."

"Ralph, stop making faces at your food."

"Cora, what a lovely brooch. I haven't seen you wear it before?"

"To hear Gabriel Heater tell it, we're facing the end of civilization as we know it. 'Ah yes. There's GOOD news tonight.' He makes the *good* news seem *bad*"

"No, no thank you. I'm really not very hungry."

"Joanna, what are you smiling about?"

"Mother, I need to go to the toilet."

"If they do another audit, by God, we'll go public and the devil take the hindmost."

"Mon Dieu!"

"If there is any gravy left, please pass it down! We didn't get any at this end."

'PARDON ME."

In the beat of silence that ensued after Ralph's apology the young members of the family turned toward his smirking face.

"OOH PU!! NOW I know what a fart is!"

The children erupted with screams of laughter while the adults tried in vain to restore calm.

Ralph was mugging and grunting and Michael had pretended to lose consciousness and slumped against his father, who was having some difficulty maintaining his clerical poise. Cameron laughed heartily and Ardath shook her head and giggled wildly. I was laughing so hard I could hardly breath. The tight invisible chord that had twisted itself around the company seemed loosened and some of the adults were relaxing, some of them even smiling. I looked up at my father. He was smiling softly, his eyes full of tears.

The family, grateful for this seasonally sanctioned opportunity to stuff themselves without fear of reproach rather than engage in any meaningful exchanges tucked themselves into Evelyn's extravagant meal. I was grateful, too. Aunt Shirley, newly converted to an obscure apostolic sect somewhat beneath the Anglican dignity of our family, nevertheless glowed with zeal and exuded an aura of serene superiority. Now innocent of the characteristic red nail enamel and impeccable makeup, she smiled a secret smile at Uncle Timothy, sharing a blissful moment that excluded the rest of the as-yet unsaved company. Aunt Jeanette was uncharacteristically quiet and enervated, while Ralph indulged in his usual kinetic antics without his parents' customary restraints.

The late afternoon sun ignited the edges of smudged crystal and silver as Edith flapped back and forth through the swinging doors to the kitchen, sweeping away the ravaged remains of the meal. Aunt Shirley tapped delicately on her glass to summon attention, momentarily interrupting Uncle Clifford's offer of after-dinner drinks.

"Everyone! Please! I... we have an announcement to make." She turned to her husband blushing coyly. I glanced at Ardath who had her head back against her chair, studiously examining the ceiling. She sighed deeply.

Faces turned and conversation faded.

"Timothy and I are going to have a baby!"

A congratulatory murmur rose and flowed back and forth around the table. The children looked bored and detached, except for Michael, who stared at his mother expectantly, as though he were waiting for more information so that he might better understand the interest generated by her announcement.

Evelyn stood, smiling and clasping her hands. "Oh, that's WONDERFUL news, Shirley! Congratulations to you both!" Well! Isn't this wonderful news!" She scanned the table beaming.

Clifford rose, his flushed, moon face split in a grin. "Well! I think this calls for a drink! Everyone, what will you have?"

Orders for drinks percolated around the table as he snapped off his napkin and hurried to the sideboard. "Whoa! Wait a minute! One at a time!" His laugh echoed inside the liquor cabinet. Ardath waved her hand in the air.

"I'll have a pink lady!"

"I don't want anything, thank you, Clifford." Aunt Shirley had a serene half-smile on her lips. There were a few diffident laughs as Clifford and Evelyn brought bottles and glasses to the table.

"Why don't we all just help ourselves!" he bellowed jovially.

The company relaxed and everyone began to chatter.

"Such wonderful news, Shirley. I wish you the best!"

"Thank you, Cora. We're both very happy."

Uncle Timothy smiled with such smugness that I longed to yawn, or pick my nose, or something equally crass, to relieve the cloying atmosphere. Father mumbled something and smiled. Timothy began to speak when Michael, still waiting for some illumination asked:

"Why are you going to get a baby? You always say you have too much to do. Who will take care of it? *I* don't want a baby around the house. They smell! And they puke! Eechhh! Couldn't you give it to Aunt Jeanette? She likes babies!"

My young cousin's babble was so loud and penetrating that there was no ignoring or distracting him. Shirley, always so controlled and in command had evidently neglected to apprise her young son of the coming blessed event and prime him against any unseemly outbursts.

To the delight of the younger members, our uncle by marriage, the distinguished cleric, and his wife were intensely discomfited.

"Michael! What a dreadful thing to say! You must apologize to the family now! At once!" My aunt had lost her composure completely and was beginning to sweat.

"Why?" her son challenged. "I didn't burp, or fart, or anything!" What did *I* do??!!"

Shirley jumped up awkwardly and grabbed Michael by the hand. Happily, my cousin had been creating some sort of sculpture out of his mashed potatoes and gravy and, as is the custom of all true artists, had used his hands. My aunt shrilled and looked at her sullied hand in horror. The children immediately began to shriek uncontrollably, rolling about and banging the table as Michael defended himself vociferously. "I didn't do *anything*! What did *I* do?" He had begun to whimper and his mother, jerking him by the arm, rushed away from the table, the Reverend Timothy close at her heels. By now everyone seemed amused and unwilling to discipline the rest of the children who continued to whoop and kick the chair legs and the underside of the table. Ralph had noticed that if he kicked hard enough, the silver and flatware and condiment servers that had been left on the table danced a little jig, salt and pepper, crystal knife rest, cordial glasses and napkin rings. It was a wonderland of frolicking dinnerware, joining in the celebration of Michael's splendid *faux pas*.

The atmosphere had degenerated to the point that all pretexts and mannered behavior were abandoned and a feeling of comfortable relaxation permeated the house. We repaired to the parlor, where the drinks became more generous and the cigar smoke denser. With dinner cleared the dining room had the lonesome air of an abandoned theater, that locus of drama and revelation, where all were open to close scrutiny and criticism. I watched Aunt Jeanette as she helped clear away the remnants of the meal, moving back and forth from table to kitchen, detached and dispirited, keeping a palpable distance between herself and her vibrant, pious sister. My father, after accepting his second scotch-on-the-rocks, begged his leave and began to proffer his goodbyes. He sought me out and with attempted casualness, took my arm and guided me to the library. He cleared his throat and flushed uncomfortably. The scotch had done nothing to fortify him for our conversation.

"Jo I want you to be a good girl and help your Aunt Evelyn every way you can. I know you will. You are a good girl." His sad attempt at closeness by calling me by my nickname inspired in me a surge of pity. It seemed as though he was talking more to reassure himself than to instruct me. He sat me down on the old leather sofa and began to pace slowly, frowning and occasionally clearing his throat.

"Joanna," he began, almost formally, "it's been a while since you've seen your mother." My heart sank.

"She's better," he went on quickly. "She's much better." His voice was low and drained of life.

Aching shame struggled against my bewilderment and anger. I wanted to shout: "Don't talk to me! Stop making it seem like everything is OK! Mother isn't here! Toby isn't here! Just leave me alone. I wish you would all leave me alone!" Tears sprang unbidden to my eyes and I was betrayed. My father, as would be expected, misinterpreted my unspoken rage for sorrow. He sat beside me and seized my hands. "Joanna, Joanna, I know, I know. It's been a bad time, but it will be all right, soon it will be all right!" The more he talked the more my tears flowed and the hard anger transmuted into a dismal, cold fear. The weaknesses of the adults around me hurt and scared me and made me want to retreat into a place beyond the reach of their pity and solicitude. He hurried on, holding my hands tight.

"Next week, a week next Sunday, I... *we're* going to visit her," He hurried on, a rehearsed speech quickly delivered, leaving no space for protest or surprise. "I've already told Evelyn and Cliff that I will come by after breakfast and we'll go, just the two of us, to visit your mother. She wants to see you, Joanna. She misses you." His voice dwindled away at this last. I just stared at him, not knowing what I was supposed to do or say.

"O.K." He sat back relieved, accepting my acquiescence for anticipation, as though there was any choice on my part. He took a deep breath and rose, smiling down at me. "Now. I've got to go. Now you be a good girl, Joanna, and I'll see you Sunday week!" He pointed a finger at me and winked. His attempt to lighten the atmosphere embarrassed me and I turned away, nodding numbly.

"There's a good girl!" A quick kiss on the cheek and a pat on the arm and he was gone.

I continued to sit, steeped in gloom and loath to join the rest of the company, trying not to think about the projected trip to visit my mother. The last time I had seen her she was being restrained, screaming and crying like a wounded animal. Frozen in disbelief, I had watched with an almost perverse, detached curiosity as they pulled her away from me. Someone had wrapped a gray blanket around her; her hair was loose, flying about her head, reminding me of a picture of a witch I had seen once in an old book. The last thing I remember hearing her say was: "No ... no, it can't be. It can't be." Then they half-carried her, struggling and weeping, to a big black car. That was more than a year ago; I hadn't seen her since. I thought of the sea, and the crowd that called out in shrill staccato voices to me as I turned and ran toward the waves, past some people dragging a boat onto the beach and a group of curious children, gathered, staring, murmuring and pointing. I ran into the water and someone grabbed me from behind and pulled me back. Someone shouted "Get the little girl. Get her." Blinded by my rage, I kicked and screamed until my throat hurt and I began to throw up. Someone said "I think she said something about 'going to get Tobiska'? I don't know what she means. Take her up to the pavilion." The world turned from white to black and everything stopped.

I must have slipped off the couch and was sitting on the floor, my arms wrapped around my knees. Cameron was crouching down in front of me.

"Josie, Josie, Josie. Come back. Come on back."

My mind swam back to the library and I focused my eyes on my cousin. I shook my head. Was he coaxing me back from my visit to the sea or did he want me to go to the sun room with the rest of the children, bickering and clowning. I caught glint of concern in his eyes and shook my head, which had begun to pound. Spirals of light ignited the corner of my eye and part of Cameron's face disappeared.

"I'm going to my room. Tell Aunt Evelyn ..."

As I got to my feet a rush of pain made me stagger. Cameron reached to catch me and I hurried past him, nausea and dizziness almost overwhelming me. I must have gotten upstairs and to my bed without incident; I don't remember. The holiday was over.

"You haven't had one of those in a long time now, have you?"

So immersed was I my remembrances that it took a moment to bring me back in the present. I paused, looking out across the lake. We sat on a slatted bench, legs stretched out, John's left arm entwined with mine. He was straightening the cuff of my sleeve, looking at it as if with some interest.

"A couple of months ago. When you were in Rochester. I spent most of that weekend in bed." I unwound my arm from his and leaned forward, resting my chin in my hands. There was a covey of brants circling about on the far edge of the water, clucking and murmuring to each other, occasionally turning and plucking at a shoulder or preening a wing. A breeze scuffed the surface of the water and a single willow leaf twisted down and settled on the dark pulsing surface of the lake.

"They'll be off for the Carolina coast, or the Indies, or somewhere, vacationing away from their cold lonesome homes."

John was silent. I turned and caught him watching me with some curiosity. "What?!" I sat up straight, feeling slightly defensive.

"I didn't know you'd had another headache while I was gone; you didn't say anything." he said slowly.

I shrugged, not wanting to talk about it anymore. People were either irritatingly solicitous or righteously critical of my headaches. The sympathetic were uncomfortable and clumsily intrusive and the critical were sure I was either hopelessly neurotic or self-centered or both. I didn't want sympathy or judgment. When a migraine struck all I wanted was to retreat to a quiet room, away from the insistent sounds of a demanding world. "It had already gone. I felt better. Anyway, what difference could you make?"

"I sometimes feel I never do make a difference." I turned to look at him, surprised. He had gotten up and started to walk quickly coward the hotel that sprawled behind us, all turrets, angling wings and verandahs surging with people revelling in the gift of a preternaturally balmy October day. I rose and ran after him.

When I caught up to him, I determined to distract him. A bit breathless I began to chatter about being hungry and trying to remember a place just down the road where they had wonderful food, where we had gone as undergraduates, eating and drinking far into the night He walked on silently, occasionally glancing down at me with an "I-am-not-amused look" that only served to challenge me further. I began to babble about the haunts of the mountains and how you could get lost, really lost, if you weren't with someone who knew their way around, if you know what I mean. He suddenly stopped and glared down at me.

"You know, Joanna, you really have to decide whether you want people to know you, or keep them at arm's length, prancing around like a clown, distracting, breaking whatever I—people feel about you. It's getting *really* tiresome, I mean REALLY tiresome. So why don't you cut back on the crap and be real!" He turned and walked away leaving me standing on the path, stunned and hurt.

What had I said? What did I do? Tears sprang to my eyes. I angrily turned away resolved that he wouldn't see how he had hurt me. How dare he? After all I had been through, after all I had told him. I nursed my rage as I quickly traced my steps back along the path down to the lake's shore. I flung myself onto the bench, hurting my back and intensifying my anger. Some of the brants had hopped upon the bank and were pecking about for morsels left by wanderers and strollers. I watched as they clucked and whistled to each other. Their lives are simple. Why can't our lives be simple? It seemed as though every time my life became more promising, something happened, someone left, or hurt me or disappointed me and I was left alone in my lonesome little world, without hope or love. I began to cry in earnest, tears streaming down my face, my nose running. I didn't care how I looked or who saw me. If anyone had approached and asked if there was anything wrong, I would shout at them and send them packing. The whole goddamn world could go away; I would fly away with the brants to a lonely sea island and live on grain and weed among the excreta of all the sea birds of the hemisphere. I began to laugh. What a baby! Goddamn it, what a big, goddamn, idiotic baby!

I leaned my head back and closed my eyes, listening to the sounds that surrounded me. Someone on the verandah laughed and far across the lake a kingfisher cried and plunged into the lake. The wind hissed in the trees. It sounded almost like the withdrawal of a wave from the sand. What would happen, what would have happened if the stretched, attenuated wave had withdrawn and never come back? Left the beach to dry, returned what it had taken, allowed the sun to put the world back together, to restore my family and my life? What if, you goddamn idiotic baby? I opened my eyes to the blazing sky and I remembered the Sunday we visited my mother. The sky had looked like this, with wispy mares tails above our heads and mackerel clouds building up to the north. But that had been in December, and it had been cold.

Excerpt from Jo's Journal, December 6, 1941

Dearest Journal:

I have neglected your horribly, dear friend. Last weekend was just terrible. I was sick the whole time. Anyway, after Thanksgiving I was sick and all I wanted to do was sleep. The whole family tip-toed around me as though I was dying, and that was alright with me. Janie wasn't at school last week, praise all the angels and saints. I think she was sick or something. I hope it isn't anything very serious, it would be wicked of me to wish that on my worst enemy, which Janie is, but it would be nice if she were as sick as I was last weekend after the Holiday. That would be OK because it would mean that she would get better and not die. Maybe throwing up and having diarrea (sp?) and not being able to go to school. Yes, that would be just fine with me.

Last week I worked very hard at my studies because I didn't want to think about going to the hospital to visit Mother. The sisters said I was one of their best pupils and Sister Damien gave me a gold star on my French exercise. I also didn't have to do any of the clearing up after supper or help in the kitchen because I had been sick.

Tomorrow Father will pick me up after breakfast. I will try to get back to you when I come home.

Your negligent (sp?) ~~and~~ but loving friend, Joanna

We didn't talk much that morning as we drove to the hospital to visit my mother. Father had corrected me and explained that it was not really a hospital, but a rest home, whatever that was. I didn't ask because I didn't really want to know. Several months hence, my roommate at school would say that my mother was in an insane asylum and I would punch her in the nose, drawing copious streams of blood and earning for me a summary suspension and exile to Cliff House until after Easter recess.

It had seemed, in my cold childish dread, like a very long trip, burdened as it was with the fear of seeing my mother for the first time in more than a year. Father had brought a bouquet of roses and a crossword puzzle magazine. Evelyn had sent with us an embroidered nightgown and Cora a bed jacket that she had crocheted. In my imagination I had pictured my mother lying amongst snowy pillows and linen, pale and lovely; these gifts of my aunts reinforced the belief that she spent all of her time in bed.

We mounted the long, shallow steps to the entrance of a imposing building that had once been a private home. A family dispute over an inheritance had resulted in its conversion to a haven for invalids suffering from an assortment of ailments that rendered them incapable of coping with the world's cruel commerce and merciless challenges. I didn't know all this at that time. Pieces and shards of what passed as the truth were sieved and filtered through the judicious agency of adults determined to protect and the defensive shield I'd labored to build around me.

A young nurse guided us to the room where my mother stayed. She chatted brightly at us, and gave me a quick appraising glance before looking up and smiling brightly at my father. I didn't respond to any of her rather insincere questions. I wanted desperately to get this ordeal over with and to go home, back to Cliff House, to my journal and my books. We walked down a long corridor, led by the perky young nurse, who moved along quickly like a trim white sailboat in a brisk breeze. She stopped and turned, smiling brightly and holding up a restraining hand. We stopped obediently. She leaned toward a door with a tiny window and tapped on it delicately. Without waiting for a response, she opened it and tilted her head as she beamed at its occupant.

"And how are we this afternoon, Mrs. Webster?" She tripped over to a deep window and snapped up the shade. The occupant of the room winced and raised a hand to shield her eyes. "We have company, today, Mrs. Webster. Isn't that lovely?" She swept a vase containing some murky brown water and faded flowers from the sill, seizing at the same time the roses from my father's hand. I had to admire her impersonal, gracefully choreographed activity, which showed no association, waited for no response. She peeked coyly around the corner of the door as it closed. "Please don't stay too long. We don't want to tire our patient, do we?" She gave us a little moue with her pretty pink mouth and I could swear that she winked. My father looked at the door blankly. I turned to look at my mother.

She sat in a wicker chair with an afghan spread over her lap. I was surprised to see her fully dressed and awake. Her hands were cupped limply in her lap, as though they contained heavy stones. Her hair had been pulled back in a twist and there were small curls escaping around her forehead. It seemed an effort for her to breathe.

"Joanna?" I was shocked at how weak her voice was, sounding as though it came from far away, deep in a cave somewhere.

Father took me by the arm and pulled me over to where she sat.

"Eleanor. How are you feeling?" He bent to kiss her and she languidly turned her cheek and smiled, closing her eyes.

"Ted."

Father busied himself giving Mother the magazine and the gown and bed jacket. She looked at them vaguely but did not touch them. Father, who seemed accustomed to this spiritless exchange put her things in the drawer of a dresser which stood against the wall, all the while reminding her to tell the nurse if she wanted them, and if she needed anything, *anything*, she was to let them know immediately, for she was to have anything she wanted. Anything. Mother sat watching him her eyes slightly glazed and a half smile on her lips. Then to my extreme discomfort, she slowly turned and rested her vacant gaze on me.

"And how are you, Joanna?" She rearranged her hands on her lap. I tried to meet her eyes.

"I'm fine, Mother.'

"Well, aren't you going to kiss your mother?" She attempted a smile.

I walked over to her mechanically, terrified that I might cry. She turned her cheek to me and closed her eyes. There was a faint scent of talcum and empty unaired rooms about her. Now it was my turn to try to smile. Mother dropped her head against the back of the chair and closed her eyes.

"Joanna got a commendation from school. For her French." Father looked at me and smiled encouragingly.

Mother laughed a small mirthless laugh but didn't open her eyes.

"That must have just *thrilled* Cora and Evvie. *Tres bien, Cherie. Tres bien.*"

I couldn't think of anything to say so I let my eyes and my mind wander. Though the room was large and high-ceilinged, my mother and her belongings occupied a relatively small corner. Everything seemed orderly and neat but completely devoid of any feeling of personal involvement. There were no photographs or pictures and but for Father's flowers that the chipper little nurse swept in with, freshly arranged in a glass vase, there were no other flowers or plants, or anything speaking of life. My mother had begun to talk to Father and he had to bend forward to catch what she said, her voice was so low. I pushed my chair back as quietly as I could, better to move away from the dreary stagnation that lay like a pall around the stranger whom we came to see who just happened to be my mother. I watched her curiously. She was thin; thinner than I had remembered her to be. She lifted a hand to brush away a hair that had caught in the corner of her mouth. She pulled at it languidly and dropped her hand absently back into her lap. She didn't look at me at all.

Outside the window a plane tree, its bark scabby and naked, scratched its branches against the side of the building and pushed against the rising wind. An empty bird's nest was cupped in the fork of one of the branches, abandoned for the season by its recent inhabitants. I wanted to get up and go over and look out the window, but was afraid of bringing attention to myself. So intensely uncomfortable was I in the presence of my mother that I wished I could slide away from my chair, open the window and fly into the the wind that coursed unimpeded through the skeletal branches of the tree. I imagined myself sitting in the top of the tree, grasping the trunk with one hand and a wildly lashing limb with the other.

"You can't shake me loose! I laughed, exhilarated and triumphant. I wound my arm around the trunk and shook the branch. "I'm going to stay here until the birds come back to their nest!" The wind rose like a great wave and shouted at me.

"You don't belong here! Get away! Get away!" The wind boomed and pulled at my hair and skin. "They won't be back. They won't be back." the tree whispered beneath the voice of the wind. "Yes! Yes!" I shouted becoming angry "They will be back, they always come back! They must! They must!

I stood on a creaking branch and hugged the tree with both arms, as the wind howled derisively at me. I tried to reach out to the nest but the clattering tree and the whipping wind pulled together and shook me, scolding and shouting. "You must go away from here, go away! There is no-one here, no-one! New nests will be built in another tree! Not here, not here! There is nothing here! No-one! You don't belong here!" The tree and the wind twisted me around and watched my face as I began to cry "Why did you come here! Why!" The voices faded and slowed and slowed, like a phonograph record losing speed.

"Why?" My mother was crying and Father bent over her in clumsy agony, trying to soothe her. He was shaking and started almost guiltily as the door opened with a clack that reverberated through the big room. "Just go away. Go ... away. PLEASE, both of you. Go away." My mother sobbed hoarsely and Father stood, white and miserable, staring at the nurse who was standing in the doorway. He tried to stammer something about the medication, seeing her daughter after so long, or some other bumbling excuse, but the nurse was ignoring her and staring at Father. Her pert demeanor had vanished and she looked as though she were about to cry.

"On the radio! We just heard! The Japanese have attacked Pearl Harbor in Hawaii!" We're at war. We're at war!" She repeated the grim message flushed with an excitement that often seems to accompany the power attendant on the delivery of bad news.

Father just stared at her. Mother was keening and pressing the heels of her hands into her eyes. I couldn't understand what she was saying; I didn't want to listen any more.

"Didn't you hear? We're at war! We've been attacked!" The little nurse stared at him, breathing quickly.

"You'd better call Dr. Winslow. My wife is going to need some medication. Please."

The nurse turned and fled, leaving the door open to the echoing clattering hall. Father stared after her without moving.

"Get your things, Joanna and say goodbye to your mother. We have to leave." He reached for his coat and looked briefly back at his wife, who had curled up like a small kitten in the chair, sobbing and gasping.

I didn't know what to do, so I turned and said, "Goodbye, Mother, I hope you're feeling better." as father grabbed my hand and propelled me into the hall, never to look back.

Excerpt from Jo's Journal, December 7, 1941

Dear, Dear Friend:

This day is like a bad dream and I wish I could wake up from it

Father and Clifford had a big argument when we came home from seeing Mother. I couldn't hear what they said, they were in the library. Aunt Evelyn was very serious. She sent us all to the kitchen for tea so we couldn't hear. Cameron and Ardath were quiet and serious, too. I think they were thinking about our being attacked by the Japanese, and when they would get to our house, (the Japanese, I mean). Aunt Cora went to her room crying and talking about savages and murder and rapine. (Someday I am going to look rapine up in the dictionary so I will know what it means and be able to use it). I'm scared, but I don't say anything. I hate it when everybody is so secret. I want to yell a bad word like "shit" or "damn" or "hell" so that everybody would get mad and even hit me and even send me to my room. My room faces the east over the river, so I can't see the Japanese if they sneak up on us from the west. I'm going to lock my door from now on.

Later—After dinner ….

> *Aunt Evelyn is taking me to school and I must leave you, dearest friend. I will tell you all about what happened and if we have to go away to some kind of shelter because of war, I will take you with me, no matter what. Even if I can't take all my books and treasures. Uncle Clifford told us that we are at war with Germany, too. I don't know why, if it was the Japanese who bombed us. So I will watch from my window for the Germans if they try to bomb us, because they come from the east.*
>
> > *Farewell for now, Dear Journal. Keep a stiff upper lip!*
>
> > > *Your friend in tribulation (sp?).*
> > > *Joanna Webster, American*

John was standing above me, looking down into my face. I knew he was there before I opened my eyes. He gently put his hands on my shoulders.

"I forgot." he said. I opened my eyes.

He walked slowly around and sat down beside me. I looked at him inquiringly as he gazed out over the lake and reached for my hand. At a sharp command from what appeared to be the lead brant, the small flock rose with a rush of wind and splash of water. The rumpled lake smoothed away its wrinkles and the surface calmed, its serenity only occasionally disturbed by the touch of the wind.

"You know you can't get a drink at this place? Apparently, it's dry. The owners are Quakers, or something." He stared out across the lake, stroking my hand absently. "I forgot." he repeated.

I turned to him. "What did you forget? Of course, you know …." I hurried on "I could have popped a bottle of wine in the trunk, but I figured we would be able to stop somewhere and pick up a bottle."

He was shaking his head.

"No." He kept staring across the lake. "We weren't going to criticize, or pry, or well ..." He sighed and looked down, shaking his head. It was very quiet.

"I just love you so."

My tears began anew, flowing down my suddenly hot cheeks. My dear John. Dear, dear John. I turned and hugged him just as hard as I could until he grunted in protest and began to laugh. The sun, which had been dimmed by a passing cloud, burst forth, sending long commanding rays into every dark and sorrowful place, demanding joy and laughter.

I got up and pulled him by the hand.

"Come on." I commanded. "We're going to Edgecombe."

END OF BOOK TWO

Book Three

".... such perfect and abject happiness ...."

The old station wagon bounced and rattled up the rutted road as we headed toward the farm. It had rained the day before and the travel was muddy and slippery. The sun was stretching its face through the torn gray clouds, touching the dim, wet leaves tentatively, setting blurred halos around the chinks of sky between the arching trees.

Alonzo had been sent to pick me up and was accompanied by Andrew, as always, and Ralph, who had managed to wheedle his way into riding with them to the station. Aunt Jeanette and he had preceded me that summer and would be leaving after a few week's stay.

The train arrived at the station almost an hour late, service having deteriorated considerably since the beginning of the war. We didn't know how long civilians would be able to travel anywhere. Cameron told me that all public transportation was going to be commandeered by the military and we would have no gas to go anywhere. I received this grim information indifferently, feeling little impact of the outside world on my affairs. Somehow, I would get to Edgecombe; Uncle Clifford would arrange it. Good-old strong, dependable, invincible Clifford, laughing jovially, resplendent in his elegant weskit, shining gold watch and fob and redolent of Cuban cigars.

The trip had been long and tedious. My head ached and my stomach growled in protest at the prolonged fast which had been imposed by my rejection of the pitiably sparse and unappetizing fare offered in the dining car. The train slowed and I gathered my bags, scanning the platform for a familiar face. As I was helped down from the train by an avuncular old conductor, I heard the unmistakable shrill of Ralph's welcoming voice: "Joanna fo fanna, tee agga go fanna! Tee-legged tie-legged bow-legged JOANNA!" He was bouncing madly like a jumping jack, waving his arms. Beside him Andrew grinned and aped his gestures, looking up at him occasionally and signing: "Joanna, hello, hello, Joanna." Alonzo was leaning against the car, arms folded, smiling, with a cigarette in the corner of his mouth. "Hello little one!" he called. The boys popped and swirled around me as Alonzo stowed my bags on top of the car.

"You *still* haven't got it right, Ralphie. It's 'Joanna, Bo banna, tee agga fo ...'" I was interrupted by Andrew who pulled at my arm, grunting urgently. He stood straight and smiling, his eyes glowed as he signed: "Ralph and Jeanette visit." He slowed a bit as I crouched down in front of him. "We have last ham tonight. Last ham. Andrew has surprise for you." I smiled and nodded, silently signing "I love you, Andrew." He hugged me, nearly knocking me over. As I laughed and struggled to get up Alonzo opened the doors for us and Ralph chimed as he rounded the car: "Lonzo, go bonzo, go agga foe gonzo ..."

Alonzo filled me in as we rode back to Edgecombe. All but three of the chickens had been killed because they were getting old and not laying well. It was hard to get pullets for replacements since the war started. He had tried to enlist in the army and was rejected because of his disability. Not even a soft desk job for an old Indian. The last of the hams that had been smoked last year would be tonight's dinner, a celebration of my arrival. Little Sprout was doing well in school and Fantine had had another litter of kittens, this time in the loft of the barn. Only four this time. Poly the one-eyed torn was still around, but sleeping most of the time on top of the piano, and of course, Trot the dog was still chasing rats and rabbits, catching fewer all the time. The fishing hasn't been so good this year and people aren't traveling up here since the war started. Don't know what will happen, don't know how long the war will last.

As Alonzo talked, he gripped the wheel of the car, negotiating the potholes and ruts, squinting away from the tendril of smoke that curled up from his cigarette. He seemed cheerful, even philosophical as he spoke of the future and its looming shortages and insecurities.

"Can't do a whole heckuva lot 'bout it anyway, can we?" He turned, smiling, and winked at me. I sighed and settled back beside him, wishing away my headache and thinking about dinner.

Excerpt from Jo's Journal: June 28, 1942

Dear Old Friend:

It seems like in Jersey, everybody talks about the war all the time. Shortages, blackouts, etc. Up here at the farm they don't talk about it so much. They get the New York papers so they get all the news, but its like they don't think about it so much. I don't know. It's kind of a relief, in a way. At school, we pray for the boys in the services and for all the boys who have died. I guess millions and millions of soldiers will die before the war is over. The papers have stories about what is happening in Europe, how bad it is. It seems so far away, almost like a story told to scare you. Anyway.

Besides, Ralphie and Andrew are always interrupting and being rambungshous (sp?) and distracting the grownups. Alonzo calls Ralph "Mushapupik", (sp?) whatever that means. We are all trying to teach Ralph how to sign. It isn't easy. Andrew caught on real quick, I guess because he pays attention better. Andrew is funny. When he gets exasperated (sp?) with Ralph, he bounces up and down on his bottom and sort of hisses and squeaks and looks at me for help.

I have to go now, they are calling me for dinner.

Your loyal and patriotic friend,
Joanna

(I will try to find the dictionary so I can look up those words)
VEE FOR VICTORY

When we finally arrived at the farm, I ran up to Nammy and hugged her so hard she cried out with a protesting laugh and attempted to hold me at arms length, remarking on how I had grown; much the young lady now. I felt slightly chagrined, knowing that more would be expected and yet less would be imparted. I wasn't sure being a young lady was what I wanted for myself. All I wanted to do after I arrived was to go outside by myself and stretch out by the pond and watch the sky, maybe close my eyes and listen to the birds and bugs. But everyone was determined to encompass me with attention designed to distract and amuse.

Aunt Jeanette, red-eyed and tousle-haired greeted me shyly. "Hello, Joanna. We're so glad to see you. How are you doing?" She gave me a quick hug and sniffed as she turned away. "Ralph! Oh Ralph, you have to finish picking up the room." In response to a protesting whine she replied sternly. "You *have* to find the rest of the game pieces, young man, or the dog will eat them. You just keep looking!" Her voice rose, strengthing with every word, firm on the familiar turf where she did battle to her young son. She turned to me again and straightened her shoulders.

"I wish you could have stayed longer with us, Joanna. But I couldn't . . . I—I wasn't well. You understand?" She nodded miserably, trying to smile. No response was possible, so I returned her nod and smile.

More and more I had noticed that adults spoke to me as to an understanding, forgiving adult, without the slightest notion of honesty, as though I was ignorant or unworthy of candor. They were begging absolution from the wounded child before them. The insults of tragedy and grief were unendurable and therefore met with incongruous denial. Jeanette continued to smile and nod.

"Have you seen the kittens, Joanna? You *have* to see the kittens! They are just *so* sweet." She fluttered away chirping and scolding reprovals to her oblivious young son. I went up to my room, hoping to get some rest before supper.

I looked slowly around, reestablishing myself in my funny little aerie under the eaves. Outside my window a swallow had built a tough little cup of a nest in a corner beneath the pitch of the roof. The bird sat in it with her head sticking out of the little hole, her tiny black eyes glistening in the sun. Someone had tidied up a bit in preparation for my stay. The coverlet was freshly washed and mended and my old Raggedy Ann smiled a welcome from her slouch among the pillows. I took down last year's calendar and frightened a spider who raced outraged, down the wall into a crack in the wainscotting. Alonzo had brought up my bags and put them right inside the door. I retrieved my Journal and my Nancy Drews from the school bag. As I put them on the shelf, I noticed that the book of silly poems was gone.

I turned and sighed. I would unpack my clothes later. Sister Teresa and Saint Janie were not there to command "the proper attention to one's wardrobe". Let my clothes get wrinkled. Who cares? I threw myself back on my bed, closed my eyes and tried not to cry.

Just before dinner Andrew took me aside. He reminded me that he had a surprise and I was to come outside so he could show me. He kept looking around as he signed, took me by the hand and led me firmly down the porch steps across the yard which was bathed in the soft light of a waning sun. I was pushed firmly toward the swing that hung crookedly from a high branch of an ancient oak. Soberly Andy then directed me to close my eyes. I sighed, sat on the swing and obeyed. I hooked my elbows around the ropes so that I could sign to him as I waited patiently in the darkness. "What is it, Andrew? What's the surprise?" I paused and listened as he took some deep breaths. "It must be heavy." I signed and smiled. He took a very deep breath and held it. The air rang with the chipping of swallows and belling of jays. A bee buzzed by.

Back at the house someone had started to sing and Trot spoke his throaty bark. Another sound, like the fluting song of a mechanical toy, from a sounding well not deep but wide, floating and closing around the tongue.

"Yo AHNYA. Nyoahnya!"

My eyes flew open. Andrew stood before me, eyes tightly closed, his face dark and his little brown fists tight. He nodded grimly, sounding my name. I was quite dumb. I waited quietly, watching him as he stopped and took another deep breath and opened one eye. He regarded me anxiously. Did I understand? I smiled and started to sign. "Wonderful, Andrew, you are very, very smart!" He began to nod and sign so rapidly that I had to ask him to slow down.

"Joanna, teach me to talk. I want to talk!"

He looked at me, his head tilted to one side, just as Toby used to do. His eyes were pleading and he began to bounce up and down on his toes. I stared at him. He could talk; he could learn. Why *can't* he talk?

"Later." I signed and rose taking his hand to lead him back to the house. Ralph was on the porch standing on a crate and smashing at the dinner bell that hung outside the kitchen.

"Chow time! Time to chow down!" He yelled at the top of his voice.

I hurried toward the house, dragging Andrew behind me, fiercely trying to plug the hole in the ragged dam that held back my tears. I was tired of crying; I didn't want to cry any more.

"I think it's *just* adorable." Aunt Jeanette was looking at a picture in the pattern book. I sat opposite Nammy, rocking my hands up and down as she wheeled the pale, yellow yarn from the skein I held for her. Nammy hummed a little note of exasperation.

"Adorable or no, I've got to finish it before the baby comes."

Jeanette put down the book and looked longingly at the tiny sweater, stabbed with knitting needles that lay in her mother's lap. She sniffed and turned away. Nammy paused, looked at her daughter and opened her mouth to speak. Apparently reconsidering, she gave me a quick glance and continued to build the soft golden ball in her hands.

As though picking up on a mutually perceived thought or an interrupted conversation, Jeanette pushed her coffee cup slowly around and said softly "It's just that we've tried so hand. No-one knows how hard we've tried. And without even wanting to, Shirt...." Nammy quickly picked up the knitting in her lap and took what was left of the skein from my hands and addressed me crisply.

"Joanna, dear. Would you see where Ralph and Andrew have gone? I think they were headed for the stream. I don't want them coming in all wet for lunch. Jeanette? I have to go to the market. Keep an eye on the children, won't you?"

Her daughter murmured assent and left the room, untieing her apron then stopped and retraced her steps to retrieve the empty coffee cup.

I was hurrying to the door, grateful for the reprieve when I heard Nammy's voice from the parlor.

"Joanna, come here for a minute, will you?" I had an unaccountable sinking feeling as I walked slowly back to the parlor. Nammy was examining a book that was open in her lap. She looked up at me, smiled, and held it up.

"Where did you get this, dear?" My heart sank and I blushed like a guilty thing. She read from the cover: "The Nonsense Poems of Edward Lear. It's all right, Joanna. Come on over here." She patted the arm of her chair. I looked at the book in silence. Aunt Jeanette could be heard clattering dishes into the sink. Poly started from his morning nap and blinked at us from his perch on the sideboard. He stretched luxuriously and yawned enormously, unfurling his frosted tongue and closing his eye. We both watched him as he rearranged his keg-like body and coiled into a shadow-striped lump amid a constellation of exploding dust motes.

"I used to read to Toby from that book." I said. She handed it to me and I tried to give it back. She shook her head and smiled.

"Would you like to have it?" Without waiting for a response, she laughed a little and shook her head slowly. "I had forgotten about it. It seems like such a long time ago."

I sat down in the rocker opposite her and took the book, unable to refuse, and flipped slowly through the pages, catching glimpses of the antic grotesqueries of Mr. Lear's drawings. I took a breath.

"Nammy, who is Elsie Chandor?"

There ensued a silence during which Nammy gazed without expression through the arch leading to the hallway as though a stranger had just walked into the house. I slumped back in the chair wishing devoutly that I hadn't said anything. The clock clucked portentously and struck the three-quarter hour. Poly grumbled and twitched in his cat dream.

"She was your great-grandmother. Your grand-father's mother." she added extraneously.

Her voice was calm and detached. She turned and smiled at me mildly. I kept my silence unable to decide whether I wanted her to continue or not. When she did, I found I was glad; curiosity being a potent ingredient in my character.

"The Chandors were friends of the family. We had known them for years, all our lives, in fact. The great-grandfather, let's see, Elsie's grandfather, I think, yes, grandfather, was a robber-baron in a modest way made a fortune and knew how to keep it. His son pulled out of the market, he and Bernie Baruch ...." here she laughed lightly "just before the house of cards collapsed. What a mess! Jesse didn't share any of his inside information with father, unfortunately, and our investments," she made a light, graceful gesture, "gone, like a will-o-the-wisp." She sat back smiling, looking up at the ceiling. "It might have been, in fact I'm quite sure that it was deliberate, I mean on Jesse's part; we had had a falling out. The families, I mean." She was silent for a moment and then waved her hands as though brushing away an annoying insect. "It's over, all over. The past is past, and that's all there is to say." She fell silent again.

I remained silent, groping for questions in my mind that could be answered and that would not offend. Why did I think they would hurt my grandmother? It was a curious, troubling feeling.

Nammy started to rise and turned to me. "Arden Chandor was your grand-father, my husband. I left him when our children, your mother and aunts, were little. We got a divorce and I married Alonzo."

I didn't have a response, despite the questions boiling inside me. She took my arm and shook it impatiently.

"I've got to go to town to market. Check on Andy and Ralph, would you, Joanna? I won't be long." She smiled, patted my arm and left the room.

Her simple, succinct account rang with truth but begged so many questions that I began to formulate a small catalog of mysteries for examining later. I got up slowly, digesting my grandmother's momentous information and headed toward the back yard where the boys had gone to play. I could hear Ralph's shouts from the field beyond the stream where we always went to chase butterflies for pleasure and catch grasshoppers for bait. He was howling with something like rage, or joy, or triumph; it was always hard to tell, with Ralph. They were running toward me; Ralph thrashing his arms and rolling his head, Andrew behind him, imitating the older boy's gestures comically.

"OH! Oh my GOD!" he was shouting. "Oh Joanna! You have to come, quick!"

He hopped wildly across the stream on the rock bridge we had created the previous summer: a path of stones placed just close enough to let the older children cross with maximum speed and a minimum of drenching. Andrew, eschewing our rocky road, splashed across the tumbling water up to his knees, darkening his jeans and squealing with shock from the cold, still waving his arms and making little crowing noises.

Ralph stopped before me, gasping dramatically. Then he rolled his eyes and flung himself on the ground, moaning pitifully. Andrew stood over him, laughing and jumping up and down, clutching his crotch.

"You. Go in and pee." I signed to Andrew. He shrilled happily at me and ran inside.

"Get up, Ralph," I commanded in a weary voice, "before you have a fatal conniption fit."

"Oh, oh, oh! I think I'm going to puke!" I reached down and jerked him to his feet by the front of his shirt. He grunted in protest and straightened up, then went limp in a feigned swoon.

I heard the twanging slap of the screen door and turned to see Andrew running back to us from the house He had taken off his wet pants and his shirt tail flapped around his flashing brown legs.

"Yo-hannya!" He stopped and glanced at Ralph, who was now spread-eagled on the ground, gasping and making gagging sounds. Andrew pointed toward the field where the high sun honeyed the grasses and weeds of the rolling meadow that surged and fell in the quickening wind. Alonzo's big shabby dog was loping happily toward us, his silky tongue lolling out of a mouth open in a wolfish grin. I caught a whiff of old death as the wind stroked him on his back and flanks and I shouted my outrage. "Trot, you dirty old bastard! You've been rolling in deadhog again! Oh my GOD!"

Abandoning the boys, I ran back to the house, laughing happily. I turned to see my young cousin now miraculously recovered, and Andrew, close at my heels. I admitted them quickly and slammed the door, pushing the hook into place as Trot, whining and barking, hurtled himself against the bowed screen. Ralph and I flopped down on the glider which protested with a rusty screech; Andrew, from a safe distance inside the porch, signed indignantly to the dog who continued to fling himself against the door. "Go 'way, Trot. You durryobaster!"

Dirty old bastard. That's what I had said. That's what Alonzo always called Trot, despite Nammy's protests. It was then that I realized that Andrew had somehow, somewhere, learned to read lips. Maybe he could even hear a little.

Maybe.

Excerpt from the Journal of Joanna Webster, All American Girl—
June 29th, 1942.

Dear Journal and Faithful Secret Keeper:

I have decided to teach Andrew how to talk. Well, kind of talk. Because he can't really hear how things sound, or are supposed to sound, so he makes funny sounds that sort of copy talk. I don't know. Andrew wants to make it a surprise for Nammy and Alonzo, so we are not going to say anything. He told me, by signing, that he was told not to try to talk to people because he sounds so funny. Huh! Lots of people sound funny when they talk. The man who runs the stationary store in Union City talks funny because he was hurt in the war. Not this war, the last war. He had an operation and they put a metal box in his throat. Andrew has his own voice box, so he can learn. He will learn to talk.

(This is our secret, Dear Journal. A secret of both Andrew and me so it's doubly capital "S" Secret!)

Cameron and Ardath are coming up tomorrow and Aunt Jeanette and Ralph will leave next weekend. Nammy is almost finished with the sweater for Aunt Shirley's new baby and wants to mail it out to her tomorrow. Nammy tried to teach me how to knit but I don't have the aptitude. (I am going to try to use one of my new words in each entry. That's my new word of the day.)

Signing off with a capital "V" for Victory!!!

Yrs. in Patriotic Secrecy,
Joanna

Late in the summer of 1941 I was bundled off to Edgecombe for an indefinite stay.

After my discharge from the hospital where I had been taken after the accident, I was picked up by a grim, tight-lipped Uncle Edward and a weeping Aunt Jeanette to stay with them until some decision on my disposition could be made. I hated their apartment. It was suffocatingly hot and smelled stale, as though it had remained airless since it had carelessly grown to its ugly height between an echoing air shaft and the brown brick of the houses across the street. Ralph regarded me with some awe, in my new role as primary instrument of a family catastrophe.

I recalled the summer's event as if it were a dream. I half hoped, half believed that I would soon wake up in my own bed, Toby pestering me, Mother once again moving quietly around the kitchen or reading her book in the parlor.

I tried to believe there was nothing wrong with me, but I knew everyone felt that there should be, under the circumstances. My brother had died; I had been playing with him, and I thought, and they thought, that I should have taken better care of him. People watched me warily, as thought I might explode into thousands of little pieces, or fall apart: legs and arms and head bouncing onto the floor, rolling away out of the door and down the road, so they wouldn't have to worry about me anymore.

A family meeting was convened and it was decided that I should stay indefinitely with Uncle Cliff and Aunt Evelyn, so I was bustled away from Aunt Jeanette's drab home one day only a week into my stay. She hugged me and sobbed dryly, saying she was so sorry, so very, very sorry.

My father and great-aunt silently drove me to Cliff House where I would spend my intermediate life suspended between what was and what should have been. After we arrived, we went directly to my room as the strains of "Estralita" pinched up from under the closed door of the parlor where Cora had sorrowfully started the Victrola to accompany her cozily-imposed self-pity.

It was a relief to get into my own room on the third floor, away from the shock and reproach in everyone's eyes. I never went back to our house. Father and Aunt Evelyn had packed my things in boxes and awkwardly attempted to help me settle in and to arrange the little room to my liking. I asked them if they would please leave and they exchanged meaningful glances. Before she closed the door, Aunt Evelyn turned and watched me for a moment. Then taking a deep breath, she spoke in an unsuccessful attempt to reassure.

"This is your home now, Joanna. You must make yourself comfortable. We want you to know that we all love you and want to forget this sad, sad summer." Her voice broke and she attempted a smile. "If you need anything, please let me know." She watched me sorrowfully for a minute or two and I turned to look out the window. "Estralita" played mournfully in my head and I heard the door close. The tears that had not come since that awful, bright afternoon began to flow, and I curled up on the bed, my face in the pillow and wept for Toby and Mother and my empty heart.

Towering trees, gold and green, rushed toward us and sped into the past as we drove north. I was finally feeling relaxed and confident. The anticipated visit to Edgecombe, the haven of my youth, had been encapsulated in a sweet nostalgic time-warp, pristine and without remorse, incapable of reviving old hurts and sorrows. We drove in companionable silence.

Breakfast had been protracted over a much unfolded and badly refolded map as I tried to find a scenic route that would avoid the interstates and their attendant heavy, high-speed traffic. Several cups of rewarmed coffee later I bravely navigated a route that incorporated a number of secondary roads of indeterminate repair. John agreed to my plan good humoredly and I elicited a promise from him not to complain if we ran into pot holes, dead ends or the unforseen detour.

As we drove, I thought back to the last time I was at Edgecombe and of the end of the sweet, nostalgic history of our times there.

In a play, the denouement is presented to the audience in a calculated, keenly-timed construct so as to keep the observer focused and controlled at precisely the appropriate moment of the drama. This is not so in real life. Truth, or the interpretation thereof, can often be delivered at the most inappropriate moments, cutting into a scene fundamentally at odds with revelation or insight, confounding solemnity or decorum. Timing is never a consideration or guide. It is as though somewhere a God of Buffoonery waits in the wings, poised to hit us with a rubber chicken or toss a banana peel before our confident stride.

When Nammy told me about my grandfather and his mother in answer to my blunt question, a hundred more questions were born in my curious mind. Why did they get a divorce? Being divorced carried a terrible stigma in those days, the more so if one remarried. To compound her sin, Nammy had married an indian and thus was guilty of miscegenation: a fouling of the nest; marrying not only beneath her social station, but to one who was racially inferior. We came to realize this many years later. We didn't talk about it. We didn't discuss our inferiors or their strange customs and barbarities. We didn't associate with Them. Oddly, however, we were sharply discouraged from making fun of them. We knew we were superior people, and to accommodate the precepts of the True Religion that we espoused, we graciously suffered some vestigal pity for those less fortunate. To paraphrase the Saint: "There but for the grace of God go The Chosen People: Ourselves."

"When I was a child, I was quite sure the world revolved around me. Everything was arranged for my comforts and needs. Things were the way they were. We never, the children, anyway, thought to question the personal arrangements, exiles, and disapprovals of our elders. It was just the way it was. As long as it didn't disrupt or inconvenience us. Gosh! We were so damned spoiled! Yet ..." I paused, thinking, and looked over at John. "You let me know if you want me to spell you, Love." He smiled warmly.

"I'll let you know, Hon. Right now, I feel great. Any idea how much longer we have to go before we get there?"

I smiled and shrugged. I didn't even know where we were. "What time is it?" Not really needing or wanting to know.

"It's time to look for a place to eat. I'm hungry!"

Excerpt from Joanna's Journal—July 5, 1942

Dear, Dear Journal:

I know now that I have never, never, want to be a teacher when I grow up. Andy wants to talk so much and he is trying so hard that I could sometimes scream. Ardath and Cam are here now and it is really hard to find time to show Andy what he should do. I don't know! Maybe it can't be done. Maybe I shouldn't be doing this. But Andy wants to so much! I will keep trying.

Maybe if I could understand how I can talk. You know. Maybe we will have a breakthrough like they have in the war against the Nazis and the Japs. Anyway, in my Journal, I can say anything I want. I just have to be careful that no-one gets ahold of you and reads what I've written.

I will be back, Dear Journal. They want me at supper and I musn't keep them waiting.

Impatiently yours,
Joanna banana

Andy and I walked out the back of the house toward the pond, where by unspoken arrangement, our bucolic lesson was held almost every morning after breakfast. I brushed aside the queries of Ardath and Cameron who seemed uncommonly interested in my comings and goings. In past they had ignored me completely, so I imagined they would at the very least, not have missed me at all. Now it was: "Where are you going, Joanna?" "Aren't you going to stay and play Monopoly with us?" "Do you have a secret you're keeping from us, Josie?" I would ignore them and laugh, wandering casually down the back garden to the stream and over the stone bridge toward the pond. Andy hurried behind me, bounding and bouncing with uncontained joy. I would turn quickly and scowl at him fiercely and he would simply return my displeasure with a happy, expectant grin. He was hopeless.

The wind shifted and smoothed the meadow grass with a sweep that changed its color from deep green to a shade somewhat like that of an unripe pear. A large parti-colored grasshopper snapped from his perch and whirred through the air in front of us and from behind, Fantine flew in pursuit like a calico flag, tattered dugs flapping and legs lean and efficient, determined to bring down her audacious quarry.

With a few quick skips, Andrew caught up with me and smiled conspiratorally. I gave him a grudging smile and we proceeded together to the edge of the pond.

The pond was called "Samagumcookchook", or so Alonzo said. It meant "Place of the Waiting Panfish." He may have been pulling my leg. He had imparted this information so seriously that I just had to believe him. As we all had believed him when he showed us the old unused privy behind the stable. The holes were diamond shaped instead of the customary oval. He told us that it was an Indian privy. Indians, you see, had diamond shaped asses, where white men had heart-shaped asses. ("Oh yes! Next time you get out of the bath, set down on the mat. You'll see! You, and all other palefaces have heart-shaped *tocheses!*) He had explained all this to a rapt audience of young, impressionable children. That's why the white man came to America, he said. They had heard that all the savages had diamond asses! We all nodded gravely, except for Ralph, who asked "What are tookeses?" Nammy arrived just in time to terminate our scurrilous tutorial.

Andrew and I sat down on the plank that I had placed on the pond's edge and we watched the darning needles swoop and hover just above the surface and the waterboatmen dart and dance on the taut skin of the water.

I laughed as I remembered Alonzo's tall tales and Andy pulled at my arm inquiringly.

"Remember Alonzo's lessons?" I signed. Andrew laughed indulgently. He lived with Alonzo, after all, and was used to his fantastic stories.

"AAHNG-zo." his laboring little voice flat and honking. He signed "Alonzo" in translation for me. His face was grim.

I grabbed his hands and put my face down close to his and enunciated fiercely. "I KNOW what you said. You said it good!" I nodded and squeezed his hands. In frustration I took him by the shoulders and shook him. He began to keen.

I stood up and slowly scanned the mountains beyond the ridge of pines. If only I could fly; close my eyes and lift my naked, featherless body above the water, to a place in the mysterious mountains where golden eagles soared and flowers in colors never seen before bloomed in crevices riven by lightening and knives of ice. I began to walk slowly along the shore, watching the glint of the sun as it shattered across the surface where Andy had just skipped a stone. To my left a kingfisher rattled and tacked in triumph as he plunged into the pond for his lunch. Ahead of me large frog plopped into the water. I began to walk into the water, slowly, watching the mud swirl and ooze under the pressure of my feet, curling into the holes of my sandles, between my toes and away, like little puffs of smoke. I stood for a moment looking down at my slowly submerging feet and took another step. Behind me Andy began to call. I kept walking. The surface shivered and sent rings toward the further shore., Clouds of muddy water swirled around my knees and I felt the cold slap of my wet dress against my legs. I walked another few steps and shut out the sound of Andy's wails as I ducked below the surface. The water smelled like the earth of the forest, and the sharp wet skins of. fish. It was dark and the water began to feel warm.

"What happened? Where did you last see your brother?"

A man was leaning toward me, talking slowly. There was a ring of white empty faces around us. Behind us the water moaned and the air throbbed, and a woman, my mother, pushed the faces away and grabbed my arm.

"Joanna! What have you done? What have you done? Where is he? Where did he go?"

Her voice echoed against the flat faces and the wind blew the alarms of the gulls to sea as they took her away.

"I'm sorry Toby. I didn't know how much you needed me. You always needed me and kept at me and I ran away from you. Why didn't you stay with Mother and Father? I'll find you and bring you back! We'll make a new castle and dig for sand crabs and collect shells and sea glass. It was just a little while ago, you can't have gone far. Wait, Toby, I'm coming! I'm coming! Wait for me! Wait for me!"

The sea is quiet and the wind has stopped. Toby is gone. It is as though he had never been. He was so little and had been with us for such a short time. It seems as though he hadn't happened at all, but had slipped into and out of my life like a grim cautionary tale told by the thin little Irish girl who cared for me when I was little. He had been there, of course, but the soft shallow impression of his life had been brushed away by the sweep of the westerly winds and the scrubbing, scouring surf.

Once upon a time there were two people who were very much in love. Their names were John and Joanna. They went away together to a bright golden place where no-one could find them or tell them that it wouldn't work out.

Joanna was trying to live without hurt after the shock of a death and the lies of silence. John had ridden out of the West like Lochinvar, to help her and be strong for her as she began to learn how to breathe again and look up without pain. They would make a new life together and live happily ever after. Amen.

We sat close together, watching the big shimmering sun change the colors of the mountains as it slipped below the horizon. I had just told John my little story and was holding his hand in both of mine. Although we had driven all afternoon and into the northern dusk, we hadn't gotten as far as we had hoped and still were a long way from Edgecome.

"What did you do?"

"I didn't mean to scare Andy. I just didn't care. I wanted to go in the water. It felt warm, like a blanket, or arms, like a mother's arms."

He turned and put his arms around me, holding me tight. The sun slipped down behind the hills, changing the colors of the trees. We quietly held each other, needing nothing, feeling the emptiness fill up with calm and relief. In the depths of the calm, I said *I think I would like to sleep now.*

I had never seen Nammy cry. I had shunned the tears of all the others; tears that had been shed for Toby and for Mother; for fear of the war; for loss of lovers, theft of husbands, life and reason. Children can't apprehend the grief of the world until they see the shedding of tears or blood. They just know fear and abandonment, the loss of comfort, the absence of reassurance.

I never knew of Nammy's pain at the loss of her grandson; her disappointment in the daughters who had rejected her. When Cameron and Alonzo pulled me out of the pond, muddy and bedraggled, gasping and weeping, I was furious, and raged at their callus, brutal interference with me and my choice. I struggled, cursing and yelling unsupportable and unforgivable threats and accusations. Cameron dropped my arm and turned away. Alonzo squatted beside me on the grass and stared at me. He wouldn't let go of my arm. I opened my burning eyes and saw him staring grimly at me.

"Little one, little one! You made your Gramma cry. You *meshugge*? Stop that, now, stop it! Stop it!" He began to shake my arm. Never had I seen him so angry and hurt.

I stopped crying and looked at Nammy, who stood tall and stricken, her fists clenched against her face. She was gasping and her eyes were red. I scrambled to my feet and ran to her. She grabbed me by the arms, shaking, and spoke through clenched teeth.

"Joanna! Why? How ... could ... you! If you *ever, ever* . . ." She dropped her hands from my arms and stared at me. Then she swung her arm and hit me in the face, hard, with the flat of her hand. For a moment I saw an explosion of stars and felt a hot welt rising on my cheek. My ears rang and my mouth filled up. I stood, shaking, while she turned and ran back to the house. Cameron and Ardath, without a backward look, hurried after her.

Sometimes a long time fits into just a few seconds. I stared down a tunnel of sorrow toward the house, which looked very far away. The screen door was flapping slowly closed and Fantine, who sat on the bottom step, looked casually over her shoulder and began to groom a paw with her sharp efficient tongue. I swallowed a mouthful of thick salty saliva and touched the side of my face. Alonzo slowly walked away from me. He bent to retrieve his cane, shook his head, and labored up the steps of the porch.

I could not think of what I did or what would happen to me if they decided I wasn't well enough, or good enough, or smart enough to

stay at Edgecombe, where I really wanted to be. I might do something
wrong, something worse. I stood waiting for feeling, for understanding,
to return to my empty body.

A bell-like frog sound and a pull on my dripping sleeve
returned me to earth.

"Yo-HANYA, YO-HANYA? Doh .... Doh ..."Andy was
struggling between sobs and I crouched down in front of him, putting
my trembling hands on his neck. I attempted a smile; my mouth felt
swollen. Then I grabbed his hands and put them on my neck, against
a throat that still rasped with the assault of my rage and buried dread.
I began to speak slowly as an idea illuminated my mind.

"AHN-Dee, AHN-Dee" He began to nod and opened his
mouth. I put one of my hands on his throat and one on his. He
tried to smile and put one of his hands on his neck. YES! YES!" I
rasped, nodding and smiling.

'AHDEE! AHDEE!" His little mind and mouth worked
carefully as he nodded in rhythm to his voice, which became
more and more musical and clear. I stood and threw back my
head and howled.

"YES GOD, YES GODDAMN. YEEEEEEESSSSS!"

I began to dance and jump around, arms in the air yelling
and laughing. Andy joined me and chanted his name and mine
in a wonderous litany of delight. I stopped and fell back on the
ground screaming with laughter. Andy watched me laughing, then
recklessly threw himself down beside me. When he laughed I heard
the echo of Toby. I couldn't remember Toby when he was unhappy,
and when he visited me in my dreams, he laughed. I looked over at
Andy and signed, holding my arms straight up in the air.

"We did it, Andy! We had a BREAKTHROUGH! NOW . .
." I jumped up and pulled him to his feet. "We are going to read
a silly poem."

I kicked off my sodden sandles as we ran towards the house.
Before our onrush Fantine uttered a cry of inidignation and bounded
away toward the barn and her neglected, clamoring offspring.

My bath was being prepared in the summer kitchen. Ardath stood pouring water from a steaming kettle into the tub. She looked up at me quickly. "What're you doing, Joanna?" It wasn't just a greeting. I remained silent and she turned to go out to the pump for some more water. She passed Nammy coming in, who directed me with an economical gesture to take off my clothes and get into the tub. I complied quickly and silently. A fresh bar of hard blue soap plopped into the water beside my knee; I retrieved it and began vigorously rubbing it into my scalp.

"I saw you with Andrew just now. Don't know what you're doing, but I don't want *anything* to hurt that boy. You hear?"

I nodded quickly.

"I mean ANYTHING."

A deluge of luke-warm water from Nammy's big soup pot cascaded over my head, leaving me gasping and shivering. I continued to nod frantically. She seized the soap from my hand and began the most vigorous scrubbing I had ever experienced, leaving me pink as a piglet, scraped and scalded, ready for the spit. We maintained our mutual silence as Nammy completed my toilette, braiding my hair in one long plait, none too gently, either. When she finished she rose, picked up the wet towels and dropped them into the washtub.

"Don't forget, you're to set the table for lunch."

That was all. She turned and left me standing. I mutely began emptying the tub potful by potful into the deep ancient sink by the door.

"Yo! Yo! Yo!" belled from the doorway. I dropped the pot into the tub with a clang and lowered my chin to my chest. I looked sideways at "that boy", who was poking his head around the doorway where the sun glanced rainbows off his blue-black hair and nodded with him as it glinted through mellow dusty windows and the polished fixtures of brass and zinc, the silvery soap and the dirty grey water.

He stepped forward into the doorway, shoulders squared. "You promised me a silly poem." he signed.

Life goes on. Joanna might be crazy but she will not be indulged; she must take up the baton as before and resume the race. Her fragile mother had been sentenced to the tender tyranny of caretakers who kept her supplied with palliatives and placebos in an attempt to comfort a broken creature past comforting, never again capable of recovery and happiness.

'A silly poem." I signed, and leaned toward him as I ennunciated it loudly. I grabbed his hand and we ran up to the little haunted room under the eaves, where my roommate was a tiny spider and a family of swallows lived just outside the window.

Except for two days during the following week when Alonzo took him fishing out at Loon Lake, Andy and I worked every day on his new skill. He was a quick study and a dedicated student. He had developed new patience and zeal and worked by himself when I was busy with chores or sparring with my cousins in the relentless love-hate relationship that never seemed to pall. Cameron could never forgive me for beating him once at Backgammon and Ardath cleaned us both out playing Rummy. All seemed as it had been before.

I got a letter from my father who was stationed "Somewhere in England". The letter had rectangles cut out of it so that it looked something like a paper showflake badly executed by a small child with blunt scissors. He said that he couldn't tell us much about the war but that he was well and the people were very kind. The English had suffered terribly in the air raids and they welcomed any parcels we could get up for them to send through the Red Cross. He had gotten my letter and said he was glad to hear from me. That was all. That and some empty space where something really interesting might have been said. Everything was censored and I would never know all the truth that I needed or wanted to know. Cameron explained that there were spys everywhere and who knows what important military secrets my father knew that could make us lose the war if the enemy found out. I really didn't think my father was that important, even though he was a Lieutenant, an officer, not just a GI (as Cam explained to me), and in command of many thousands of men. Or hundreds, anyway. So, his tattered letter found a place in my Journal, where it kept company with some dried wildflowers and the crisp remains of a honeybee.

Excerpt from Jo's Journal August 2, 1942

Dear, Dear Journal:

It has been terribly hectic and I have neglected you terribly. Andrew and I have been working so hard to get our play together before Cameron and Ardath have to go back to New Jersey that I haven't had time enough to write.
LATER:
ANOTHER interruption. I had to go to lunch and help with cleaning. Nammy had to go to the city and we ate early. Sorry! Again! Anyway, Andy and I are going to do a little play as a sort of farewell to Ardath and Cam. It was Andy's idea, and I think he is very brave. They had better be a good audience or I will kill them. Really, I will. He is so good and we, no HE was worked so hard, it's got to be good!

Nobody has said anything about that day when I went into the pond, I guess they want to forget the whole thing. I can't really, but I have been too busy with Andy and our play to think too much about it.

I have to go now. I promise I won't neglect you so much in the future. I will see you later, dear Journal.

Love, your neglectful friend, Jo

The days passed quickly and my ideas for Andy's presentation grew so ambitious that I began to feel overwhelmed. To add to our dilemma, my young star made some demands so outlandish that had to reign him back and try to talk him out of some of his more grandiose ambitions. I frantically signed my reservations to a sulking protege who had only to squeeze his eyes tightly shut and clap his hands over his ears to dismiss me from his world. I finally decided after one stormy, tearful session that he was right, that we should have some props and some calm, rational direction. It had become evident that we couldn't proceed without help. I cast my mind about for a source of detached, mature guidance. I was immediately discouraged to realize that aside from Nammy and Alonzo, my only aid would have to come from Ardath and Cameron and I nearly rejected the idea out of hand. The prospect of asking them to help us with our little project paralyzed me and made me nearly sick.

One evening I summoned up my courage and approached my cousins, who were working on an almost completed jigsaw puzzle at the parlor table. I prayed they would be in a good mood. It always helps when begging a favor to ask of someone already feeling successful and generous. I stood silently watching them as they ignored me and pushed the occasional piece into place.

"Wow, that's good. You're almost finished." I chirped lamely.

Cam looked up quickly and then back at the puzzle, smiling with self-satisfaction.

"I could've done it so much faster if Miss Pickybritches here didn't keep knocking pieces off the table."

Ardath hummed and smiled, unperturbed by her brother's gibes.

"What's up, Josie?" Cam stretched and pushed his chair back. "I'm hungry. Josie, go into the kitchen and see if you can find some cookies or something. Well?"

I took a deep breath. "Cameron, Ardath? We need your help." They looked at me expectantly so I hurried on. "See, Andrew and I have a sort of a surprise for Nammy and Alonzo, before we have to go back, you know. Sort of a play, well, no, sort of an *entertainment*, and we need some help. I mean, we need somebody good, really smart, to show us how to do ... Ah, forget about it. It's a dumb idea. Just forget I said anything." My face felt hot. I felt a knot in my stomach and my throat began to close up. I was perilously close to tears.

There was a beat of silence as my cousins gazed at me with their cool hazel eyes, curious and detached at the same time. They looked at each other briefly and Ardath turned to the puzzle, punching in a piece with her fist.

"So, tell us about the dumb idea, Joanna," she said, smoothing the surface where she had inserted the piece. Cameron was watching me with interest. The setting sun behind them had ignited their hair with a glow that reminded me of a lovely Pre-Raphaelite illustration, full of icy beautiful knights and ladies and lush, dark, bosky forests. They were so far above me. I felt ugly and insignificant. At the same time, I didn't know whether to be heartened or discouraged by her use of my proper name undistorted by foolish diminutive or mocking doggerel.

Joanna. I was a stranger in the family. I had been brought to live in the aloof ambience of their discomfort. They had suffered the loss of a child because of my carelessness. I had caused the rupture of my own fragile home. I was constantly reminded of our loss by their looks, their sighs, their stifled tears, their silence. Maybe that's why Andrew and I got along so well. He was a stranger, too. A stranger with something missing; an embarassment to the family. They never came to see him, or invited him to their homes. It was though he didn't exist. He was the mistake Nammy had made. An unforgivable, irretrivable failure on the part of a member of our distinguished family. Poor Nammy. Poor Andy. Poor Joanna! To hell with them! Who did they think they were? I couldn't speak. I turned quickly, hurried from the room, and ran up the stairs. My cousins called after me but I blocked out their voices and gulped back my scalding tears.

My room was hot and dim. The tiny spider shivered down a thread of shining silk and sped to a dusty niche in the corner. It's better here. I'm better when I'm alone, I thought. Raggedy Ann stared crookedly at me, her rusty hair thinned with age and her candy heart gone, the dessert of some hungry mouse. I picked her up. Her dull black eyes stared back at me. Suddenly in a wild surge of righteous rage I yanked up the window and threw her as hard as I could out into the yard.

"Goddamnsonofabitchingbastardshitshitshit." I growled into the pillow, waiting for my tears to stop and the pain to go.

The room was rapidly darkening and a cool breeze quickened through the open window. A katydid scraped her song in the old oak and further into the sky a nighthawk boomed down the wind. With my face in the pillow, I imagined the beauty of the evening, cool and settling into a horizon streaked with gold and crimson. The little brown bats would be swinging through the air, gulping plentiful suppers of freshly hatched insects. The crickets sounded their A's and began a tumbling, reverberating chorale. It was that lovely, but I could not look out at it with its marvelous, generous beauty. I was unworthy: I could not forgive or be forgiven.

A rustle at the door and a soft knock brought me bolt upright. "Who's there? What do you want?" There were some indistinguishable murmurs and Ardath said:

"Joanna, can we come in? We need to talk to you." There was a soft exclamation, then a scuffle and a muffled retort. Cameron continued.

"C'mon, Josie, open up. It's getting late. Come on!"

"Please, Josie. I'm sorry. I *guess* I'm sorry, or I'd *be* sorry, if I knew what I did. Pleeeze?" I could picture Ardath jittering by the door, twisting her face impatiently.

"The door is open." I hoped I sounded firm and in command.

The door opened a crack and Cameron peered around, cautiously surveying the room. When he saw me sitting indian-style on the bed he braved a smile and opened the door all the way and gave Ardath a little shove, propelling her clumsily into the room. She gave her brother a half-hearted slap and turned to look at me, smiling tentatively.

"Hi, Joanna!" she ventured feebly.

I didn't say anything. The sun had fallen behind the hills and the room was almost dark. I reached over and turned on my bedside light.

"Josie!" Cameron laughed hollowly. "Look!" He gave Ardath another poke and she gave him a withering look. "I made Ard steal some cookies for us. There were some left after all!"

Ardath advanced toward me slowly, as though she were afraid that I might become suddenly crazed and jump at her and maybe scratch her face or pull her hair. She winced and opened the napkin that she held in her hands. There were some shards of Nammy's oatmeal cookies and alot of crums.

"I hope Aunt doesn't find out I took them, she'll crucify me!" she said in an attempt at glibness. Still, I didn't speak. They exchanged glances and Cameron sat down carefully on the edge of the bed and offered his disarming smile. I gazed at him stonily.

"Look, Josie. I'm sorry. *We're* sorry" Ardath, standing at the foot of the bed nodded energetically. "I ... we hope you're not mad at us." He put away his smile and looked serious. "It's just that, I don't know, you've been sort of funny lately, you know, I mean not funny, More like secretive, You know? And, well, we felt, well, sort of left out. Do you understand?" He paused, looking at me earnestly.

Ardath hesitantly approached and put her peace offering ceremoniously on the end of the bed and backed off, smiling timidly. I had to suppress a laugh; she looked as though she were about to curtsey. For a little while there was silence.

I slowly stretched out my legs, watching them watch me.

"You know what?" I asked in the softest voice I could manage. They looked expectant. I took a deep breath, compressed my lips and nodded. "You know what?" I repeated. They shook their heads solemnly.

"You are both so full of shit."

There was a shocked silence. I leaned back and watched them. They were too stunned to exchange their usual complicit glances. I swung my legs over the edge of the bed and stood up. They followed me with their eyes. I felt energized and very eloquent.

"You only play with me when you have nothing better to do. You think I'm a little pest. You really can't stand me. No, wait." I stopped their protests. "You don't like it here, you think it's boring and you take it out on everybody. Well, I don't like you either. What makes me mad is that Andy *does* like you. He likes everybody. He's just a little kid and doesn't know any better. But you look down on him. He's not one of *us*. He's different; he's a freak. He's an Indian who isn't an Indian, because Nammy is his mother, and Nammy is US. Not only is he different, he can't hear. I guess you think it serves him right, being a half-Indian and not an "US" I had begun to nod righteously, arms folded, cheeks flushed. I was warming to my lecture. My cousins remained frozen, shocked to watch their very own family worm turn. I walked toward them slowly, they shrank back and I couldn't help it, I started to laugh.

"Andy CAN talk. I'm teaching him, and he wanted to make a surprise for you and Nammy and Alonzo and recite for you." I felt tears begin to well up, ready to betray me and spoil everything. I made a concerted effort and swallowed hard. "He's doing really well. He's *very* smart. He can read and write, and alot of kids his age can't even do that. Now he wants to talk, like you two, and maybe, just maybe he'd be accepted. Excepting he'll never really sound right, because he can't hear himself talk." I stopped in frustration. I needed them to know what a great kid Andy was and how he wanted their approval and admiration, just like everyone does. I sat down hard on the bed, miserable and hurt and looked out the window. I didn't want to see my cousins anymore but I couldn't tell them to leave.

I felt someone sit down beside me. I kept staring out of the window where the fireflies winked and a katydid sawed away at her song.

Something ticked out in the night and I desperately tried to recall my words, but couldn't clearly remember what I had said. My mother had once told me that saying hurtful things was like driving a nail into a board. You could pull the nail out, but there would still be a hole, a permanent wound. Never could you call back your words; the damage was done. In my fevered unhappy mind I felt I could never be forgiven.

I was spared continued agonizing by Ardath, who came up with the most banal response anyone could possibly imagine, and I was heartened to the point that I felt almost fond of her, she of the overweening vanity.

"Well! Josie! We didn't know you felt that way about us!" She sounded surprised, rather than hurt, and I was further relieved. I turned to Cameron, who was sitting beside me on the bed looking at me gravely. I tried to smile and immediately abandoned the attempt as a bad job.

"Balls, Ard! Why shouldn't she hate us? We're sucking little bullies and it was great sport to torment her." This time it was my turn to begin a protest and he waved me to be quiet.

"Shut up, Josie. Good for you for giving us hell. And I won't tell Aunt that you said shit if you won't tell her I said balls." He paused looking very serious and we suddenly both began to howl with laughter. Ardath began to simper behind us and finally started to laugh nervously, obviously not enjoying the joke as much as her brother and I did.

We laughed until we sobbed with exhaustion, flat on the bed, spreadeagled and sweating. Ardath looked down at us, bewildered, but smiling in the knowledge that somehow, everything was going to be alright.

'NOW!" Cam jumped up, startling us both. He rubbed his hands together. "What are we going to do to get this show on the road?" He turned to me inquiringly. For the first time in our short, uncomfortable, on-and-off lives together, I saw respect in his look and began with great energy, to explain what Andy and I were doing. Ardath joined us on the bed and listened wide eyed, injecting a question here and there.

We would have talked and argued far into the night, losing track of time, but for a call from the landing which brought us back to the present. Ardath and Cameron immediately rose and started quickly for the door. Cam turned and signaled me to be still and winked. I felt, for the first time in a long time, perhaps ever, that I was being welcomed and accepted.

"What's this?" Alonzo was puzzling over a slightly battered package that he had brought in with the mail.

We were sitting around the breakfast table trying to keep our anticipation in check, occasionally giving one or another member of our conspiratorial team a knowing look, trying hard not to smile or appear anxious. Not a great deal got past Nammy, however, and she watched Ardath and Cameron and me with a slight smile and a small frown. Andrew had become still, sensing something in the charged atmosphere. He looked to me for an explanation.

"What happened?" he signed to me, a puzzled look on his grave round face.

"Nothing. We'll talk later." I attempted to be casual and perhaps overdid it a bit because I got a kick under the table from Ardath, who had entered wholeheartedly into the game.

"Isn't this the package you sent Shirley? Looks like it didn't get there." Alonzo turned the package over in his hands. "Pretty dumb, I think." He shrugged and handed it to Nammy, who looked as though she were about to speak to us about our strange behavior. I was momentarily relieved and made a face at Ardath across the table.

Ardath rose and began to clear the breakfast things. I sensed Nammy tensing and heard her quick indrawn breath. She turned quietly and walked stiffly out of the room. I followed her, a sinking feeling in the pit of my stomach. When I stopped in the doorway I collided with Alonzo, who was right behind me.

"You go on, little one. I'll be with your Gramma."

He spoke very softly and I slipped back towards the hall. As I turned the corner I looked back and saw Nammy holding the little yellow sweater in her hand and a letter in the other. Her face was quite red and she was trying not to cry. Alonzo put his hand on her shoulder and she shook it off impatiently. Without a word he sat on the arm of the chair and put his arms around her. I heard her crying softly as I hurried back to the dining room. Andrew was waiting for me, sitting on his chair, swinging his legs.

"Well?" He shrugged, hands up, eyes wide. His gestures spoke for him; there was no need to elaborate by signing. I watched him for a moment my head pulsing with anger and pain and fear for Nammy. I could only push my horrid imaginings to the back of my mind, where they kept jostling and slipping back to take over my thoughts and immobilize me with emotion. I took a deep breath and reached for the little boy's hand, gesturing "let's go" with my head.

We walked together into the yard as far away from the sounds of weeping as I could. The birds called and sang, not knowing that there was sorrow so near. The sun cut sharp bright shafts of light through the sheltering oak, whose leaves whispered back to the soft wakening wind. *Please be kind. Please be still. Someone is sad, something has been lost. Hush now! Hush!*

I looked back at the house, listening. Far away I could hear Ardath and Cameron clattering and arguing in the kitchen over the washing up. There was silence from the front parlor. I turned to Andrew, who had sat down on the swing and was twising himself around and around. I grabbed the rope and bent down: "ANdrew?" He looked up at me and smiled, put back his head, closed his eyes and spun around and around dizzingly until I had to turn away. I heard him laugh as he dragged to a stop and wagged his head at me.

"Andrew. Andrew. Listen to me." I spoke slowly and distinctly. "We need help for our play. There is too much for us to do." I took a deep breath. "Cameron and Ardath want to help us." I began to sign frantically. "It will be good to have them help, we *need* help!" I had grasped his upper arms and spoke in a slow, urgent voice. He considered me soberly for a long while, then turned his eyes to the left, then the right, seeming to consider. He looked at me and nodded.

"HOKAY." he spoke and signed, mimicing my earnest manner.

A flood of relief rushed over me. I grabbed him off the swing and ran back to the house, dragging the protesting little boy behind me. "It's Hokay, Little Sprout. We're going to have a conference. Like the presidents and the generalissimos and the prime ministers have to get the war over with!" I knew he couldn't hear what I was saying but I was full of enthusiasm, a serious hurdle cleared and a smooth track ahead.

We entered the kitchen and marched straight to the sink where my cousins messily labored. I was definitely in charge. Ardath and Cam paused and looked at me inquiringly. "Andrew has given his hokay. We can start the campaign at oh-one-hundred hours!" I smiled triumphantly and gave a smart salute. Ardath and Cameron returned the salute and Cam bent down and gave Andy one of his own. Andy smiled, snapped to attention and returned Cam's salute. We were ready to begin.

Autumn was peaking and the trees had begun to loosen their grip on the masses of golden and scarlet leaves they held. Occasional insistant winds combed through their crests, pulling away a leaf here and there, tossing them like pale coracles on the tides of the northern currents. The sky curved like an azure dome above the arching mountains and glass-green and silver-blue waterways.

John and I had stopped overnight at a small guest house west of Saratoga where we had been served with a lavish breakfast and a hefty side-helping of local lore ("You know, General Grant had a place just up the road.") and weather forecast ("Going to be another beautiful day!"). Eager to be on our way, I promised rashly to return for another visit to their charming house, and yes, we had slept very well, and no, I couldn't eat another bite. I waved, smiling and hurried to the car while John dealt with the bill and loaded our bags into the trunk.

On the road north I watched the passing towns and the mountains surge up around us feeling oddly serene, free from anxiety, relaxed and calm. I looked at John who turned and smiled at me.

"That was good! I'd go back there again." He laughed. "I've never stayed at a place where the cat slept with us and got us up for breakfast." We watched the road unfurl ahead of us, cutting through the mountains, rising perceptably. North and up, we traveled, into the sky, into the future; and I remembered the past.

"I wanted to kill her." I finally said.

"Who?" John was shocked.

"Shirley. My Aunt Shirley. I wanted to pull her hair out. Scratch her face until she bled. Bend her fingers all the way back, one by one, until she screamed. What a horrible, self-righteous bitch." I stopped, shuddering. "When I came back to the house after our meeting, I went directly to the parlor where Nammy and Alonzo had been. What a little sneak I was!"

The air thrummed around us as the wind rose. The boiling, thickening clouds reached around the sun, covering and stripping the air into flashing ladders of shadow and light. A hawk gyred into the blue, so high it was lost to our vision.

"Our exit?" John asked, as though I had said nothing. I nodded and gave him a reassuring smile. He slowed and turned into the secondary road I had earlier identified on the map. Almost home. Almost back in my past.

There was silence for a few minutes. I went on.

"Nammy had crumpled up the letter and thrown it in the waste basket. It was so mean and cruel I was almost sick. Shirley said that she couldn't accept anything from Nammy, her mother, after what she had done: left her lawful husband, gone off and lived in sin with an Indian and had a half-breed child. It was an abomination and she should pray to God and Jesus for forgiveness, because she could never forgive her. Words to that effect. The letter was enclosed with the little sweater and Nammy's note, which she hadn't even opened."

"Oh Jo. That's horrible. My God! How can anyone do that to anybody!" John pulled to the side of the road and reached for my hand. He looked at me closely, his eyes full of sympathetic pain. I smiled stiffly.

"You knew I came from an odd family. Just judging from the few you've met. I guess when shock comes upon shock, people like them don't know how to react and give pain for pain." I shook my head. "Toby's death was galvanizing for me. In a strange way, it helped me survive the strange sterile life I led. The same tragedy that strengthened me burned my mother to a crisp. I can't even remember what she looked like. Poor mother!" I sat up quickly and combed my fingers through my hair. "Come on! Let's take a walk!"

The upper Hudson looks very much like every other mountain stream, cutting its way out of a place with the wonderous name Tear in the Clouds and moving imperiously through old hills born of the ice age toward the world's most celebrated port and into the Atlantic. But no other mountain stream is silted with the folklore and fables unique to its valley; depository of dreams and repository of memories personal and collective, as is our river. We walked for a while beside the shore where the water tumbled over gigantic slabs and clumps of sandstone, shale and granite shot and veined with quartz, detritus strewn by the melting ice as it withdrew and fed the rushing freshets with its dear, pristine essence. I imagined this moment of water, hurrying and slowing, rushing and crashing, pushing at the shore as it rushed downriver, I saw boats with little white sails sitting like preening shore birds on her breast; the heavy, slow barges and the hulking rust-black freighters as they moved toward her mouth. The same water I wept into flowed finally to the island city to slap and slide around the tar-blackened wharves, greasy and gleaming with the oil of rainbows.

"We used to watch the shad fisherman from the top of the palisades at Cliff House. In the spring they'd spread their nets to catch the shad as they migrated upriver. They'd stand in their little boats, fixing the poles that held the nets, then row away to wait for the fish to come. It was my favorite sign of spring. Better than the snowdrops or crocuses. Better than the first robin pulling her first worm. Better than rubber baby buggy bumpers. Better than the opening of Palisades Amusement Park. Well, *almost* better."

"Tell me about your triumph with Andrew. I'm sure you bullied your cousins and changed the family forever." John was watching the river as it splashed and swirled into little pools in the rocks before it clambered out to join the rest of its rushing body. I bent down, picked up a solitary red leaf that trembled at my feet and dropped it into the stream. Some poignent lines, recited so long ago by my mother, returned to me:

Dark brown is the river,
Golden is the sand
It flows along for ever;
With trees on either hand

Green leaves a-floating,
Castles of the foam,
Boats of mine a-boating—
Where will all come home?

"We had fights. I cried. even Ardath cried. Andy got mad and ran away to who-knows-where to sulk. Cameron yelled, we all laughed and I had to talk him out of commandeering the bathtub in the summer kitchen and painting it green with whatever paints he had stolen from wherever."

On goes the river
And out past the mill
Away down the valley,
Away down the hilt

Away down the river,
A hundred miles or more,
Other little children
Shall bring my boats ashore.

— Robert Louis Stevenson's A Child's Garden of Verses, "Where Go the Boats."

John reached out and took my hand.
"It's time to get going." he said.

We had had a particularly stormy session and I called for a time-out, or recess, or truce, depending on individual perceptions. It had been raining and was trying to clear, with the help of the wind and a pale pinkish sun smouldering through the spent clouds. I flounced into the parlor where Nammy had retreated, no doubt to avoid the children, who had, by this time of the summer, must have begun to irritate. Looking back, I found her patience wonderous, even saintly. One of an analytical of cynical turn of mind may have said she was overcompensating. I say she was just being Nammy: my wonderful grandmother.

She had just put aside some mending and was rummaging around in her basket for something. "Sun's out, Joanna. You children can go out to play." It was as close to a plea for our dismissal as she ever came. I ignored her request.

"Nammy, if someone does something or says something dumb, and everybody else thinks it's dumb, why doesn't that person change and agree with everyone that he is dumb?"

She smiled and retrieved the little yellow sweater from the bag and examined it dispassionately. I suspected she wasn't going to answer me. Still, I stood quietly, waiting to see what she was going to do. She nodded and took her scissors and made a small cut in the neck of the sweater. Curiosity rooted me to the spot. Suddenly she began to tear the sweater apart, first into strips, then strands and began quickly cut the rest to small pieces. I cried out in protest and she glanced up at me and began to smile.

"It's all right, Joanna. If somebody does or says something dumb, it's not your problem. If you have to be with that person, well, you have to learn to compromise. If not " she shrugged and looked through the window, into the past, through the breaking sunshine, watching something I would never be able to share, be it joy or pain. Her life was her own; I was only a small part of it. She returned to me.

135

"Now!" I stood ready. "There is an onion bag. They're in a drawer in the summer kitchen." She raised her voice as I turned to go. "Be sure to get a small one! Smallest you can find!"

When I returned, she was sweeping the remnants of the little sweater into a pile in her lap. I stood looking down at it. She had worked at it with such love. I remembered the sweater she had made for me, now long outgrown and sent, I am sure, to Bundles for Britain, to warm some little English child huddled in the ruin of her London home. Tears of nascient sentiment and self-pity pricked at my eyes and nose. For the duration of the war and beyond I would associate handknit clothes with loss and hurt. Nammy smiled up at me.

"Thank you, dear, that's perfect." She began to stuff the bits of wool into the orange-net onion bag and smartly tied the black string at its neck. "Let's go." I followed her obediently.

I followed her through the summer kitchen, past the tub of recent contention, and out the door to the stoop. She reached up and hung the bag from a nail and turned back to the house I stood, mystified, hoping to figure this out by myself, and not press her further. I heard her as she returned through the kitchen. "Jo? Are you coming?" I was at her heels, following close behind.

I heard Ardath and Cameron arguing from where they sat on the porch swing, which screeched painfully as they moved back and forth.

"Did."

"Did not."

"Did so."

"Didnotdidnotdidnot!"

"Didsodidsodidsodidsodidsosososososo!"

Nammy ignored them and motioned me to look at the apple tree that stood outside the parlor window. "Look. Do you see that? Up there. Look closely." She whispered, her head close to mine. I glanced at her quickly. Her blue eyes looked intently up at the tree. She moved my shoulders and tilted my head to look up. "That little nest, up there!" She laughed lightly. "Those little birds do such a wonderful job making a home for their young!" I hitched myself up on the window seat and peered into the tree. At last I saw the nest, empty now, but still cupped securely in a fork of the tree. "What do you see, Joanna?" she asked.

"A nest."

"What else? Look closely, now!"

I squinted my eyes tightly. Crisp dry grass and twigs had been woven and tucked into place by the industrious robin, the imprint of a thousand generations of skill and instinct, for one season's rest and the rejuvination of the specie. Something gleamed, shut off and on, as the sun blinking through the cast of cloud caught its shining surface. And around it wound a filament of silver punctuated by a small knob of lead. I looked at Nammy, puzzled.

"They are very resourceful, the birds. *That* is a bit of tinsel from last year's Christmas tree. I thought we had retrieved it all.

And that, see? Right THERE. Right next to it. See? It's a piece of 'Lonzo's or somebody's fishing line. They use anything and everything!" She stood up straight and took a deep breath. You see what we're doing? We're helping this year's fledglings by giving them something to build their new house with!"

I stared at the nest. A small willow switch, swollen with tiny buds had been woven into a collar that perfectly circled its edge. The grass and the tiny feathers that lined it trembled in the wind. It was open and empty like a wondering mouth; tufted with moss, tart dry herbs and old grey flowers. I didn't know what to say. I understood, and I didn't want to spoil our understanding with words. I turned, head down, and hugged my grandmother hard, rubbing my tears into her apron and closing away her laugh in my heart.

That moment signaled in me new strength and confidence. I couldn't remember ever being that happy and buoyant: suddenly awake to a feeling of limitless ability to change, and to change things with zeal, without the slightest qualm of self-doubt.

This birthing would carry me on its crest for a while; I was drunk with awareness and nascient understanding. The wisdom of the world was mine, and though I would in my bewildering and imperfect future come to grief on many occasions, I had been infused with something that would help me survive and laugh at myself and all the obstacles strewn before my stumbling feet. In future I would, in Nammy's words: "come a cropper" more times than I could count. But it no longer mattered. I was alive and strong.

I returned to earth and my self-assigned task of impresario, teacher and miracle-worker. Now I would make it work.

END OF BOOK THREE

Book Four

"…. in the most translucent and satisfactory manner …."

These mountains had been formed in the ages of iron and chaos before time began. A leviathan came down from the pole, molding the swollen body of the land; scraping and mauling, goudging and clawing as it died. As I looked at the hills spreading before me, wave upon wave to the horizon, I could almost hear an eldrich cry of rage as this terrible power was burned away by the sun. Thousands of lakes had been scooped out of the earth by knives of ice and filled by sweet springs and glittering rain.

John and I were still short of our destination by miles and paths that had begun to jumble bewilderingly at the edges of my mind. There were roads that looked familiar, only to turn a bend and reveal a odd little town, one I was sure I had never seen before. Flashes of rememberances accompanied the loamy smell of the woods and piney pungence of the evergreen uplands.

Here I was suddenly reminded of the place where the accident happened so many years ago. Ralph had begged Alonzo to take us to where " all those people died in the car crash when they went over the cliff! Please, please, Alonzo!" Alonzo finally agreed, grudgingly, and the children piled into the station wagon and we headed out, peering from the windows, looking for the odd traces of blood and twisted metal. We were horrid little ghouls, vicariously thrilling to the anticipated sight of violence and death. We arrived at the site after a good half-hour's drive and Alonzo pulled to the side of the road. He sat wordless; the car idled, bouncing softly and coughing occasionally. Ralph voiced our surprised disappointment.

"Aw gee! Is that all there is? Aw gee!! This,stinks! GEE!"

The low metal barrier that edged the curve of the road was bent and scraped where it had been hit by the car before it went over the edge. There were two or three saw horses with DANGER painted on them and a couple of round sooty-black kerosene "bombs" stuttering orange flames.

"Boy! This stinks! This really stinks!" Ralph continued his litany of indignation.

Alonzo showed remarkable restraint as he pulled back onto the road and flicked his cigarette out of the window. He didn't say anything. I looked back through the rear window as we left and thought of the people in the car: how long had it had taken to go over and were they afraid? I thought of the men in the bridge tower across the river from the Palisades. And I thought of Toby.

No, this wasn't the place, but one very much like it. The hills laughed down at me.

"It's *deja-vu* all over again. But it's *faux deja*; the *vu* is new and strange. I think we're lost." I giggled. "*Ish kabibble!*"

John shook his head and laughed. "That's what I love about you. When languages don't suffice, you make up your own."

"Ah, John! What a day! Let's never go home!"

"OK." he smiled and nodded. "But first you have to tell me about the show. Went off without a hitch? You triumphed, of course!"

"Of course." I replied.

From Joanna's Journal—August 21, 1942

Dear Journal:

I know you will understand. I want everything to be all right—perfect, and I am afraid something will go wrong. Alonzo told me an Algonquin word: "farposhkit". It means all messed up or something like that. I am so afraid that our play is farposhkitted. Maybe I made a mistake asking Cameron and Ardath to help. They have some good ideas, but nobody wants to do the work and we all end up fighting. Most of all I don't want to give away the surprise. No. Most of all I want Andrew to do this right and make everyone surprised and happy. He has been very quiet. Must go.

Nammy is calling us to lunch.

> *In haste, your loving friend, Joanna*

Later:

We have had a change of plans and I have to take charge. Cam and Ardath have to leave on Monday because they have to go away to school before Labor Day. I can stay until the first of the month.

SO.

I have decided to let the Bossy Twins take care of the props, sets, stage decoration etcetera. I will work with Andrew and if the show flops, well, we tried. We will put on the play Sunday night.

It can't flop. I'll kill myself.

> *Yours, Joannabanana*

PS—I think it's Algonquin.

I had decided that we would announce our plans for that evening's "entertainment" at Sunday breakfast. I had prompted Andrew to try to be as off-handed as he could with Nammy and Alonzo so as not to tip our hand. This would be an even more demanding role. For a five-year-old with all the energy and anticipation that had been generated in our weeks of work, it was almost more than could be borne. My confidence was beginning to flag and I guess we all had some stage fright. Ardath was snippy and nervous. Cameron seethed with the contained rage of a petty tyrant; I decided to leave them to their own devices and not even ask if we were ready for a dress rehearsal.

We had been rehearsing, for security's sake, in my little room in the attic. The cramped quarters and late-summer heat contributed to our short tempers and discomfort; thus, we ended up cutting some corners which, if properly attended to, might have made for a smoother final performance.

We were putting in yet another run through on Saturday afternoon, with Ardath improvising the background music by humming and tapping out the rhythm of the piece she would playing on the piano. I devoutly hoped that her piano playing would be more on key than her singing voice. She had contrived to put some practice in when Nammy and Alonzo were not within earshot. Even when they did hear, I don't think they suspected that something was being planned for their entertainment. I think Nammy was a little curious about her niece's fresh interest in the keyboard after months of ignoring it, but wasn't sufficiently suspicious to pry. Bless her.

"It's OK, OK. Let's just get on to the next part." Cameron had somehow taken over the job of director and was beginning to betray his mounting anxiety.

We were hot and itchy and very cranky, constantly carping at one another and finding fault with anything anyone did. Sometimes it seemed that Andy was the calmest, most mature of us all.

"Let's take a break." I let out a breath and flopped down on the bed, closing my eyes in a signal of dismissal. Cam and Ardath took the hint and quietly left the room. Their voices buzzed down the hall and stairs as they resumed an argument they had begun earlier in the day.

It was a source of wonder to me that my older, smarter, more sophisticated cousins had become so immersed in a modest presentation put on by their little cousin, ordinarily beneath their notice (or so it seemed) and their aunt's young son. Yes! I wanted to shout. Andy, also known as Little Sprout, half-Indian half-WASP, is your cousin, too! Old distinguished family: Mayflower, DAR, Colonial Dames, SAR and all the rest of it. Only *his* father's people, Alonzo's ancestors, met the boat and helped them survive their foolhardy pilgrimage into the wilderness where they planned to build the New Jerusalem.

"You still here?" I droned and opened my eyes. Andy was bent over the book of poems, reading and nodding his head at each word. I reached over with my foot and nudged his knee. He smiled to himself and kept on reading.

I tried to relax and think of something besides the project that had obsessed me all summer. I thought of other summers, other places. Cliff House, where I managed to get away from everyone in my attic room overlooking the great river and the wondrous city. When I returned in September, it would be like a different world. Everyone was closer to the war in Jersey. The blacked-out city slumped eerily against the sky at night, like some dark giant sleeping restlessly beside the flowing water.

Clifford had volunteered for the Civil Defense Corps and became an air-raid warden, complete with tin hat and binoculars. Every evening he scanned the sky for enemy planes and met with like-minded volunteers to discuss strategy and exchange confidential information, not to be repeated to a living soul, about the conduct of the war.

There were shortages and grumblings about food and gas rationing. We were sustained in our comfort by Aunt Evelyn's judicious shopping and jolly little Victory Garden near the edge of the wall, with its brave slender rows of beans, peas, lettuce, tomato and corn. She cared for it herself, fretting over the rabbits that gorged and the moles that undermined her vigorous industry. When we returned to Cliff House in September, we would be regaled with dramatic tellings and retellings of her adventures and misadventures as brave, patriotic farmer, doing her bit to help in what was referred to as "the war effort."

At Edgecombe there always seemed to be plenty. The table was supplemented by fresh and preserved foods put up from the bounty of lavish gardens, fish and venison fresh or smoked, an occasional snared rabbit or fowl, and up to this summer, the generous produce of Nammy's chickens.

I felt Andy lie down on the bed, very carefully so as not to disturb me and perhaps be banished from the room. I smiled to myself. My mind flew back: past the river, over the cliff, above the rumbling city to the oceanside and those gone forever.

"Toby was alot of fun, Andy. He used to make me laugh, and read the silly poems to him. Sometimes I would try to hide from him and he would wander around the house calling me: (JoBISka! Where ARE youuuuu? I'm going to FIND you!' I would scrunch down in a closet or in the pantry and hold my breath so he couldn't hear me when he came close. He had yellow, yellow hair. So different from yours, and he had the bluest eyes. Mother said he got his eyes from her grandmother and his name from her grandfather. Toby is a nickname for Tobias, you know. Tobias. An old, old name. It's from the Bible. But we always called him Toby. *I* called him Tobiska. From the Pobble poem, you know." I paused, watching the ceiling, watching the crack that looked like a hand pointing, or a river, or road going over the mountains, or a face in profile, laughing or screaming. "When we went to the beach that day, Toby was so excited. He wanted the water to be back so he could show us how brave he was and run into the waves."

The room was quiet. Andy was lying beside me, arms to his sides, chin up, watching the crack in the ceiling with me. He must have known I was talking because he had become sensitive to what I had learned were the vibrations and tiny movements we make when we speak. He knew I spoke but didn't look at me, even when I turned to see what he was doing. I resumed my perusal of the river, or hand, or face on the ceiling. Outside the windows the swallows chirred and cheered as they sickled through the air in search of insects. The screen door slammed and I heard Alonzo's short choppy voice and Trot's answering bark.

"I was jealous of Toby when he was born. I don't remember a whole lot, but I remember being unhappy. My mother was so pleased with my new brother, as they called him. She looked so beautiful with her long brown hair and she smiled alot. They told me that she was very weak so she didn't have any time for me, so began to hate the new baby.

"Did you know that Nammy taught me how to tie my shoes? Mother wasn't well, and father was away on a trip. Sometimes Aunt Evelyn, you don't know Aunt Evelyn, would come over and take me out to the playground or for ice cream. Nammy was staying for us for a while to help mother ..." I paused then, suddenly remembering, something that had seemed strange and puzzling at the time; something I had *decided* to forget, I think. There are some things you need to forget and there are some things you decide to forget.

I was alone in my room, coloring, I think. Mother and Toby were napping and Nammy was doing some housework; I could hear her singing as she worked in the kitchen. The doorbell rang and I got up to see who it was. Everything was so boring now that there was a baby: be quiet, go on up to your room and play with your dolls, or something, just to get rid of me. Someone coming to visit meant a break in the monotony and maybe even a present for me, because people who brought presents for the new baby usually brought something for me, too, just so I wouldn't get my feelings hurt. I went out to the landing and watched as Nammy came down the hall from the kitchen. She opened the door and started back, as though something had scared her. Aunt Evelyn stood smiling and just behind her like a dim shadow was Aunt Cora. Evelyn's smile faded. "Is something wrong, Annie? What is it?" She turned in confusion and looked at Cora, who began to stammer something. Evelyn was in command. "Annie," she turned back and reached over to take Nammy's arm. "It's all over; it was long ago. Let bygones be bygones. Annie!" Nammy had gently taken Evelyn's hand from her arm. "No. No, Evie. I don't think it's a good idea." Cora had turned and was hurrying back to the car, shouting over her shoulder: "I told you Evelyn! She doesn't understand' She can't understand' It was a stupid idea! Stupid!" This last was said with such vehemence that Aunt Evelyn started back from the door and flushed deeply. "Annie, I . . ." she pleaded and Nammy softly closed the door in her face. I quickly turned and hurried back up to my room. I was afraid to look out of the window at my departing aunts and afraid to go downstairs to my grandmother. I picked up a red crayon: CRAYOLA, it said. I began to peel the paper away from its waxy body. I remember now: it was a Mickey Mouse coloring book. I began to color Mickey's pants. I decided to forget.

It was very quiet. So quiet that I could hear Andy's short shallow breathing beside me.

It's over. All over. The past is past, and that's all there is to say.

But is never all over, is it, I thought. It makes us what are, how we think. It's still in our heads. We may think we have forgotten, but it's still in there, like the hole in the board left by the nail. I sighed again and turned to Andy. He was watching me, waiting.

"You would have liked Toby." I said.

Andy raised his brown arms and signed toward the ceiling, watching the river, or the hand, or the laughing face.

"Toby wet his pants."

I waited a moment, paused and raised myself on an elbow.

"You remember." I said, without signing. "The day in the woods we first saw you. I thought you were a forest spirit, a child of the Wendigo, maybe Little Sprout's greatgreatgreatgreatgreat GREAT grandbaby!" I laughed and nodded, signing: "Yes. Toby wet his pants."

After a quiet moment Andy sat up and turned to me, very seriously and signed. His face had darkened and his eyes were bright; he breathed deeply, not risking the sounds of words.

"I will be your brother, Joanna."

I stared at him in silence and he looked at me, dismayed.

I grabbed his hands and tried to smile, nodding. "Yes, Andy, you *are* my brother!"

He smiled shyly, mirroring my nods and opened his arms.

"Ladies and Gentlemen, if I may have your attention please for an important announcement!" I had risen from my chair at the breakfast table and waited for silence. Ardath nudged her brother who was trying to shove Trot out from under the table and beamed at me expectantly. Nammy turned toward me and smiled. I cleared my throat portentiously. My face was hot and my hands clammy. If this is the way I would be just asking them to come to the show, how would I be at the actual presentation? I shook myself and attempted to smile confidently.

"To celebrate Ardath and Cameron's return to New Jersey and St. Cuthbert's Academy for Backward Children and Hopeless Juveniles, and to express our thanks for the hospitality shown to us all by Nammy and Alonzo Twofeathers and their family, we will make a show for you all in the parlor this evening after supper, promptly at eight. I thank you."

I couldn't resist a bow, so I got a spattering of applause and a few hoots and whistles from Ardath and Cam. Nammy smiled at me, then at Andrew, who was pretending not to be excited, lips compressed and eyes rolling around toward the ceiling. We quickly rose and began clearing the breakfast things. Nammy and Alonzo had wisely decided not to ask any questions and quietly left the kitchen chores to their uncharacteristically zealous young guests.

The die is cast; my moment of truth; there is no turning back.

I repeated all the cliches I had ever heard in my head as I balled up the table cloth and headed for the back porch where I would shake it out. A small clutch of chickens greeted me expectantly. I always made sure there were some scraps and crumbs left in the cloth for them.

"Tibbie! Baby! HENrietta! Cukukukuk!" I called to them as I flapped the cloth like a triumphant banner. The hens zig-zagged up to me frantically on their little yellow-wire feet and answered: "Cukukukukukukukukuk!"

Sometimes in dreams, I find myself in a place that I know; a city, a small town, a seaside village. In these dreams I have a feeling of familiarity that reassures and guides me. These places are vivid and specific: but I have never been there before. I am confident, somehow, that just around the corner and down a short cobblestone road there is a bakery with a green and white striped awning. I am quite sure that down a columned esplanade beside a green-grey ocean there is a grove of knotted trees and a spit of land made of gigantic rocks where a boy crouches quietly, tending his fishing line. But I was never there. Where are these places of dreams? Will I ever go there? The last hour of riding was just such a dream place. Were we nearing Edgecombe at last?

I had begun to experience the drowsy indolence that sometimes sets in at a certain point of a prolonged journey. Not just the semi-hypnotic state imposed by days spent as a passive traveler borne along winding roads and rising hills, but the unexpected dis-ease brought while retracing familiar paths through a skein of poignant memories.

We had made reservations at an inn which had at one time been what was called an "Adirondack camp". Built by a wealthy New York family in the latter part of the nineteenth century, it was actually a lavish summer home, fully appointed with extravagant faux-rustic amenities and up-to-date conveniences. The vacationing Family members wanted for nothing in the way of creature comforts in this forbidding wilderness, at least by a late-Victorian standards of comfort. Much of the original furniture that had been retained were made of intricately twisted branches and great slabs of wood, polished and waxed zealously to a glowing finish. The excentricities of these constructions offered only marginal comfort to persons of the mid-twentieth century who expect more ergonomically forgiving chairs with conforming upholstery. One did not rest too long on a chair or bench; one paused for a brief ceremonial sit, to satisfy tradition and curiosity.

These grand old homes were situated in prime locations on lake or mountainside in the lee of the prevailing summer breezes. This particular inn was on the shore of a lake as clear as glass, reflecting the towering gothic spires of evergreens, the gold birch and aspen and the crimson oaks and maples. Its quiet surface was occasionally disturbed by an errant waterfowl, dropping onto its undulant surface, sending shivering ripples to smear and tear the bright mirrored reflections.

After we had checked in, John and I held a short conference and decided that this would be our last day of searching; if we couldn't locate Edgecombe by the next day, we would begin our return trip.

"We can always come back and try again."

The present innkeepers had maintained the integrity of the building; the only obvious gesture towards modernization was in the plumbing and electrical wiring. The dining hall was beamed with oak darkened by years of oil-lamp fumes and hearth fires and was hung with chandeliers made of antlers. Massive heads of moose, elk and deer gazed down on us balefully: triumphant trophies of long-past hunting parties, the pride of masculine strength and power. The room echoed softly with the clatter of silverware on china and the chatter and occasional laugh of dinner guests. John was perusing the wine list and I was lazily assessing our fellow guests and the sumptuous appointments of the room.

"We *must* come back here! John, look! See that soigne woman over there, see her? The one with the cleavage and the red sandles." I bent forward and hissed. "She doesn't know it, but there is a spider, coming down from its nest in that moose's nose. And it is going to land right on her salad!" I stabbed a finger toward my shielding hand. "She will scream and sob and ask for another table/GARCON! Hurry!' I flapped my hands in mock distress.

John picked up on the drama and bent forward, eyebrows lowered. "I am *so* sorry Madame. This spider was unaware that you had reserved this table. Permit me to move it to another table. Under the elk, perhaps? Hummmm?"

"Nonono, it will never do. I cannot stay a minute longer in a room with that loathsome creature." I threw my scarf dramatically over my shoulder and flung my head back. "Garcon! Champagne, vite, vite!"

We both sat back giggling like naughty children, pressing our hands over our mouths and bobbing our heads. The waiter, unsure of the meaning of our pantomime, glided to our table and tilted his head inquiringly.

John raised his hand imperiously. "Veuve Cliquot, garcon, and an extra glass for Arachne!"

I was laughing helplessly, but the waiter didn't turn a hair. He smiled mildly and backed smoothly in the general direction of the bar.

"You are right, you know," I said calmly. "We have to go home."

My companion smiled and leaned forward, resting his arms on the table. "You are going to tell me about the show." he said and sat back, arms folded.

"Yes, I promised."

The next morning, I woke to an overcast sky and high wind that brushed the trees steadily as it moved out of the north. The air had become noticeably cooler. It was as though the elements had all conferred during the night and decided that we had had enough, and that we should return, expectations unfulfilled and questions unanswered. *Go home* something said. *Go home where you belong: there is no-one here; they are all gone.*

I remembered the wind's message the day my mother dismissed father and me. Go away: I don't want you here. It is too late. I looked out at the lake, ruffled and scraped by the wind; the trees tilted and swayed, humming their diurnal music. I forced the window a bit and propped it open with a book that someone had left at our bedside. A cool gust of wind puffed into the room and I heard a loon cry and laugh at the hills.

My heart and thoughts were far away, laughing and crying with the loon when I felt warm arms close around me from behind. *I really think I might go crazy without him* I thought as he nuzzled my neck and shoulder. *Drink heavily or, at the very least, become an obsessive spinster, like Cora, disrupting dinner parties and hording contraband pornography in my dresser drawer.* I giggled and turned to return my lover's ardent hug.

"Cora caught me one day." I interposed. "I had gone into her room, just for a minute; it had such a ... an ultra-feminine atmosphere." I shrugged and struggled to find words to describe the elegant boudoir of my great aunt. "Anyhow, I opened a drawer, lingerie, it turned out to be, and lo and behold, beneath some lacy camisoles and corsets, was a plain brown envelope. Yeah." I nodded and chuckled with John. I was having some difficulty relating the story between kisses. I would rather have been kissed, but was determined to finish my pathetic little tale. I twisted away from him and fell back on the bed.

"She came in and almost screamed when she saw me." I remembered the scene and its dreadful, shameful confrontation. "She called me some terrible names, or at least terrible for my innocent young ears; she sputtered and choked and cried. I felt horribly guilty, as though they were *my* dirty pictures, and that *I*, somehow, was tainted. Oh sure, I shouldn't have been in her room, and I really wasn't spying or trying to hurt her, but she made me feel so ... so wicked." I kicked my legs and stared at the ceiling. I was recalling my hasty apology and flight from her enraged advance when I was pounced upon by my lover who wasn't at that moment particularly interested in the crotchets of my odd family. It was quite a while before we resumed any discourse.

At breakfast we briefly recapped of our itinerary.

"What are these?" John interrupted.

"Cream scones, I think." I answered, swallowing a mouthful of eggs benedict which had been presented lavishly garnished and snuggled in a cradle of some kind of frilled purple leaf. I had been ravenous and my moment of esthetic admiration was defeated by a hunger sharpened by the morning's energetic love making.

"Don't you have scones in Ohio?"

"Skuns?"

"Oh, OK. That's what the family called them. SCONES. I laughed. "I used to go up to Edgecome saying things like 'scuns' and "LYbree" "and I went home to Jersey at the end of the summer saying things like 'schmuck' and 'privvy' and..." I turned my fork in the air, searching my memory "... and, YES! Wanabitanookie', the legendary Algonquin wise woman who lived somewhere up above Old Forge." I shook my head and returned to the happy task of ravishing my breakfast.

"Cream Scones." John held one up and examined it minutely. "'What are these things, raisins?" He plucked some bits out of the piece he was eating.

"They're currants." I leaned toward him and began to laugh. "My first dirty kid-joke! Did you hear the one about the Dugan man who was electrocuted? He sat on a fruitcake and a currant went up his ass!" I laughed heartily as I once had as a nine-year-old. John stared at me smiling and shaking his head.

"What's a Dugan man?"

"Oh my GOD! Is it so long ago? The Dugan man was a bread man. He came to the house and delivered bread and coffee cake, things like that. I don't think there is any Dugan bread anymore.

Gosh! That dates me! Or maybe you just didn't have Dugan men out there in that benighted place you come from." I nodded hopefully and returned my fork to its proper function, scraping with great energy the the last bit of egg yolk marbled with hollandaise sauce.

"Wonderful!" I smiled down at my empty plate; breathing a small prayer of gratitude for a morning crowned with the happy satisfaction of appetites.

"Wonderful." John echoed.

"Let's go." I rose briskly. "We'll talk when we get on the road."

Excerpt from Jo's Journal August 23, 1942—afternoon

Dear Old Friend:

I have just talked with Cameron and he seems calm and collected, as Uncle Clifford says. Ardath is nervous. Who would have thought it? Little miss I-know-everything and I'm-better-than-anybody! Anyway, Andy seems, very calm and told me he doesn't want to practice any more. So all I can do is check the scenery and props. Ardath is practicing on the piano. It sounds better than I thought it would. It sounds better than her humming anyway!

I will be glad when this is over, old friend. This has been very fatiguing (I love that word. It is so much better than tired) Andy and Alonzo are fishing in the pond and Nammy is out getting whatever is left in the garden to make some soup. I will report on the big First Night before I retire. (Retire: doesn't that sound better than go to bed?)

Your faithful friend and constant companion.
Joanna

P.S.: Don't say a word! "Loose lips sink ships!"

The late sun was pouring into the parlor, touching with light our little proscenium. Together Cameron and I dragged in the green-painted corrugated box that stood in for a boat and an draped an old sheet over the bookcase as backdrop. Nammy and Alonzo were directed to chairs placed just in front of our improvised stage. They settled down with self-conscious clearing of throats and tentative smiles. Whatever the outcome, I was sure they would be pleased, or at least patiently amused. Ardath settled herself at the piano, cleared her throat theatrically and wiggled her rear. She placed her fingers on the keyboard and executed an arpeggio, then turned a pert look over her shoulder. She had regained her composure.

Holding Andy by the hand, I walked to the front of our stage. Andy shuffled sideways a bit, looking to see where he was supposed to stand. Looking straight ahead and smiling brightly, I nudged him a little with my knee and we bowed simultaneously. There was a spatter of applause and a murmur of approval from our audience. I released Andy's hand and realized that I had forgotten every word of the speech I had memorized. My eyes swept over the heads of Nammy and Alonzo, along the library table and the wing chair with its little side table and floor lamp. Outside the window the leaves hung heavy in a late-summer weariness, as though anticipating the tingle of changing color and draining life. A branch shuddered as a robin rose from its perch. Time passed and I forgot my fear. I looked down at last at our audience. Nammy was leaning forward anxiously and trying to smile. I grinned.

"Ladies and gentlemen. Thank you for coming to our Summer Theatre presentation of The Owl and the Pussycat.' Our reciter will be Andrew," I flourished my arm back to Andy, where he rose from the chair he had been sitting in, nodded his head, and sat down quickly, "and he will be accompanied by Miss Ardath Charlotte Ashburn at the piano. The decorations and background have been made by Mr. Cameron Thomas Ashburn, and I will assist Andrew." I faltered. "Thank you. We hope you will enjoy the performance." I quickly moved back to where Andy sat and experienced a sudden surge of panic.

Ardath struck up "I Am the Captain of the Pinafore" and Andy took center stage. I had never felt such love and pride before and at that moment nothing in the world mattered: not that I would have to go back to St. Anne's, not for all the admiration and respect of my cousins, not even the winning of the war and the return of our boys, safe and sound, meant as much to me as this little boy's success.

He bowed once and we all applauded. He turned and marched behind the cardboard boat, reached down, then stood, holding over his hands the puppets we had cut, sewn, and glued to resemble crudely, but unmistakably, an owl and a cat. He looked at them both seriously, joined them in a bow. Nammy murmured a motherly murmur; Alonzo chuckled.

Andrew turned to me and I smiled, nodded, and raised my hands. He took a deep breath.

"THOU ahn duh fuh-seeca wendo ZEE inuh beufoo peereen BOW"

He moved his puppets in a rocking motion, his eyes darting from me to his little audience. I signed the words, nodding encouragement and trying not to look at Nammy.

"Dey toosumunny anh blennyuf munny hurrap of inna fipow NOTE!"

Andy knew the poem by heart. He had read it over and over again, all by himself, trying to make the sounds that he had seen me make to match the words. The sun shifted a shrug away from him and he neatly stepped sideways to stand in its yellow spotlight. Ardath slowly began her Gilbert and Sullivan medley, glancing over her shoulder occasionally, nodding and smiling encouragingly at the little performer. Suddenly his words came to me clear and clean, without the thick chime of his raw new voice in an aging young throat. The words rang to me happily above the tinny music and I signed frantically to keep up with him.

"'The Owl looked up to the stars above,"
(Cameron "backstage" shook the curtain spangled with yellow-crayoned stars)
"And sang to a small guitar . . ."
(The twang of an untuned ukelele was heard from behind the trembling stars)
"O lovely Pussy, O Pussy, my love, What a beautiful Pussy you are,
YOU ARE,
YOU ARE!
What a beautiful Pussy you are!"

His cheeks were flushed and he seemed to ride along on a quickening crest of excitement, all but ignoring his audience. The hand puppets banged together in joyful loving hugs and he giggled happily at his clever improvisation.

"Pussy said to the Owl, "You elegant fowl,
How charmingly sweet you sing!"
(An offstage, off-key warble bubbled up and down the scale and was mercifully stilled)
"Oh! let us be married; too long we have tarried:
But what shall we do for a ring?"
(The tinkle of a handbell was heard from backstage, a pun insisted upon by Cameron against the objections of both Ardath and myself)

— The title, the aphroisms and poetic fragments throughout the text and, (of course) "The Owl and the Pussycat" are from The Nonesense Poems of Edward Lear.

I winced and watched Andy as he made his puppets shrug and shake their heads. I turned toward the audience and looked at Nammy. She was staring with a strange, striken look at Andy. She rose slowly from her seat and stood quietly until he stopped his kinetic ad libbing. He looked at her curiously. Ardath stopped playing and slowly turned about on the piano bench. Alonzo looked quizzically up at his wife. "Annie?"

Nammy pressed her hands together and looked as though she were about to cry. I was suddenly confused and helpless. I stepped forward. "There's more." Andy turned toward me, looking for direction and Cameron poked his head out from behind the curtain, eyes darting about. Nammy interrupted.

"That's enough, Joanna. Thank you. I think that's enough." She was clasping and unclasping her hands and her voice was strange and thick. "Very good, children. Thank you." Then she turned and hurried from the room.

I felt hurt and shocked, without any idea of what to say or do. Andy was looking at me with an expression of mixed surprise and anger. The sunbeam shifted again and he turned away from us and walked out of the parlor. I sat down on the nearest chair exhausted and sickened. I wanted so much to cry, but the tears that had so often betrayed me by their unwelcome intrusion, this time deserted me. Andy's spotlight had faded and slipped to the sideboard where Poly napped, dusty and unconcerned.

"Don't stop! I know this place! Yes! Just a little way down this road, there is a side road, driveway, really, and then .... don't stop, John!"

He had turned to the edge of the road and pulled the handbrake on fiercely. He stared straight ahead, face rigid.

"John?"

He began to shake his head. "You poor kid. You poor sweet, dumb kid."

"You could say that. Yes."

We sat quietly for what seemed a long while, then he shook his head. "You dear, sweet, dumb, innocent ...."

"Oh shut up John!" I said cheerily. Let's get on with this ride. We're almost there! Come ON!" I leaned over and gave him a large grapplingly childish hug and loud kiss.

He turned and watched my profile for a brief moment. "There's more, isn't there? There had goddamn well better be a happy ending!" He pulled back on the road, shaking his head while I smiled and snuggled against his side.

"Just keep driving 'til I tell you to turn."

"Yes, boss."

I knew exactly where we were. The turn was the same but the trees stood taller, shaking loose their last season's leaves and lifting bare limbs of welcome. The brush that carpeted the wood was more overgrown and tangled than I remembered with clumps of rusty fern, fragrant bayberry and flames of virginia creeper licked up the bark of trees frosted green and silver with lichen.

"The last time I was here ... it must have been ... Here! Turn here, John! This is the drive that goes up to Edgecombe, I know!"

I was both terrified and exhilarated, knowing that I could be cruely disappointed. At the same time I felt oddly detached, knowing somehow that this confrontation with my past could be cathartic. Nothing fraught with such powerful emotions could live up to its history and the mythology that I had dressed it in. I felt the vulnerable child again. I wanted to stop and turn around. I also wanted to hurry faster so I could see the house, the swing, the porch with the bell, the pond.

John must have sensed my anxiety and the need for haste. He bent forward over the wheel and pressed down on the gas. The road was narrow, deeply rutted and grown over in spots with tangles of weedy saplings and tough vines. I wondered for a moment if there was anyone or anything there anymore. I closed my eyes and put my head back, whispering a silent prayer for I knew not what: release? revelation? restoration?

"There's a clearing up ahead. Yes! There's an old house. Seen better days, I think. Looks empty."

I squeezed my eyes tight, afraid to look, afraid of the ghosts that wouldn't be there.

John slowed the car and stopped.

I opened my eyes.

Ardath and Cameron, in remarkable show of discretion, had begun to dismantle the set and gather up the props with as much dispatch and stealth as they could manage. I watched them quietly for a moment. As she left the room Ardath glanced quickly over her shoulder at me with an expression of pity approaching real sympathy. She was human, after all. Or almost human. Cameron gave her a sideways shove and mumbled something about her fat arse. She gave a brief soft whine and they were gone, leaving Alonzo, the exhausted, devastated shell that had once been myself and Poly, who mumbled and shifted langourously in his sleep.

"That was good, little one. You did good." I forced myself to look at him. He sat back in his chair, hands clasped on his knees. He smiled a little and nodded. I looked away. The house pulsed with guilty silence. I strained my ears for some sound of pain or anger; there was nothing. Alonzo smacked his hands on his knees.

"Let's go outside, it's nice out. Come on!" He stood up and waited and I dragged myself to my feet. My resentment, fueled by the shock of the evening's events, began to burn. I walked stiffly past him out into the hall and through the door, slamming it hard after me. I didn't look back to see if he followed.

The sun had sighed and withdrawn behind the trees, blinking drowsily and diffusing the air with a sandy afterglow. My swallow was darting and looping about in pursuit of the last insects, old, drugged and slowed by the implacable progress of the season. Her nestlings had long since fledged. One day I would wake and she would be gone, her nest hollow. Like my heart. Now my tears could start. There was nothing like a little self-absorbtion to prime the pump.

I walked slowly to where Andy had made his secret fort, past the garden, near the edge of the wood. When I had first stumbled upon it, he made me swear a solemn oath to not say a word about it to anyone, even Nammy and Alonzo. He had balanced a plank of plywood on two large rocks to provide a small cave that he had carpeted with pine needles and hemlock boughs. It was so small that he had to crouch down to get in, as little as he was. I tipped the roof back and looked inside. I had to laugh through my tears.

With Alonzo's discarded scraps of wood, Andy had created some very imaginative furniture: a table and two chairs, which were constructed of irregularly shaped chunks of wood and sticks. He had even made a bed with an old moth-eaten Indian blanket and what appeared to be some potato sacks. On the table was a candle stub in a cup and some books. On the bed was my Raggedy Ann, stained and faded, and nearly bald. I picked up the ravaged doll that smiled at me with a crazy broken grin, and I remembered throwing her from my window in a fit of temper, and with a pang, how I had not missed her. Suddenly feeling intrusive, I replaced her gently on the bed, folding her hands in her lap. She was Andy's now I turned to leave and the books caught my attention. I knelt down and began slowly and carefully picking them up in turn, as a guilty intruder might. There were some comic books, an old Farmer's Almanac from 1940, and a notebook with a marbled black and white cover. On the tide space, printed in bold capital letters in red crayon it read:

ANDREWS JERNEL—STRICKLY PRIVATE

Andy had seen me writing in my journal; he must have known that I wrote things down when I was alone. He had watched me. I remembered his coming in to my room earlier that summer. *What are you doing? he had asked. I'm writing in my Journal, Andy go away! This is strictly private!*

I rubbed the drying tears from my face and nose and looked at the doll tilted against an old needlework pillow.

"This is a strickly private jernel, Raggedy, and you know what? I'm not going to read it, even though I want to." I placed it firmly back in its place on the table and arranged the comic books and the Farmer's Almanac on top of it. "Besides, I prolly couden unnerstan' his ritin' anyways." I smiled and nodded at the doll and she smiled crookedly back; her missing shoe-button eye winked at me.

As I carefully slid the roof back on Little Sprout's inner sanctum, I felt for the first time some relief from my bewilderment. *Oh Andy!* I thought. *Oh Toby!*

Alonzo was standing at the edge of the pond. He must have seen me at Andy's cave and stayed just far enough away so that I wouldn't notice him. He was smoking a cigarette and poking at something on the ground with the tip of his cane. I walked slowly and casually towards the pond and stopped, just far enough away so he'd could see me but not close enough to have to talk. I crouched down and sifted through the grey pebbles on the shore's edge, looking for a good skipping stone. A crow shouted *Back! Back!* I stood and listened as Alonzo walked over to where I pretended to scan the sky for our wishing star. We waited quietly for a moment. Then he spoke.

"Where'd you get the idea, Little One? I mean like the play, and all." There was a beat of silence. I could hear the smile in his voice. "He's one smart little guy, that Andrew. You can bet your life on that!" he chuckled, and I skipped my stone. It touched the water four times as it flew across the surface, then was swallowed at last by the hungry pond near a shaggy clump of cattails.

"It was Andy's idea." my voice was low. I bent down and scrabbled around in the stones again, feeling strangely guilty, as if I had blamed Andy for something that I had done wrong. I stood.

"I mean, he *wanted* to talk. He wanted to be like everybody else. *Say* stuff, you know." I felt hot, my anger returning. "And he *can*, too. You said yourself. He's *smart!* Smarter that that dumb Ardath! She thinks she knows everything! She's just a fat, dumb *paskudnik*"

An explosion of laughter from Alonzo startled me so that stepped back and turned away to hide the nervous smile I felt starting behind my face.

"Oh Little One! You're so funny! No wonder Andy thinks you are the best thing in the world! Paskudnyak! Oh my God!" He sat down heavily and leaned forward, laughing helplessly. I wavered between frustrated indignation and the need to share his joy, finally succumbing to hysteria, bewildered and infected by Alonzo's high spirits.

We laughed until the shock of humor exhausted itself into gulping gasping, teary trickles.

"Oh dear, oh dear, oh dear" said Alonzo.

"Oh dear, oh dear, oh dear, oh dear" I replied.

The sky was alight with an afterglow that looked like the inside of an old rainbow. A few sparks flew across the water as the sun tried to grab at a handful of pebbles I threw into the pond. The swallow swooped and soared and cheered over the pond and into the sky to try to catch the newly-wakened evening star.

"You wanna hear a story, Little One?"

I nodded, relieved, and sat beside my old friend.

He cleared his throat and gave a low whistle through his teeth.

Long long time ago there was a man that could send his eyes out of his head send them up to sit in a tree, then he'd call them back: "Come on back, eyes!" And they'd come down, and POP! back into his head they went.

(OOh that's disgusting!)

This is a true story. Told me by my Grandfather Watching Foxes and told to him by his grandfather long before the Trail of Than, so it is a true story

(Go on. But this sounds very strange.)

Anyway, White Man sees him do this and he yells: "Hey I want to do that, too! Show me how to do that." So, the man taught him how to do it but warned him: "Never, never do it more than four times a day because if you do, they won't come back any more." So White

Man went away very happy because now he could send his eyes out
of his head But, you know how White Man is, he ignored the man's
warning. He thought he could do it as many times as he wanted, and
one day after the fifth time he sent his eyes up on the tree limb, they
wouldn't come back. They just sat up there, staring down at White
Man. He called and called: "Hey you, eyes, come back down here!"
But the eyes just looked down at White Man and stared at him like
this, and just wouldn't come down. White Man begged and begged,
but the eyes just stayed up in the tree. It's not funny!

(Sorry!)

White Man called and called, but the eyes just sat up on the tree
and wouldn't budge. After a while, the eyes began to swell up and
spoil like a dead groundhog laying all day in the sun, and all the flies
came to set on them. You gonna be sick?

(NO!)

You got a funny look. You know? So anyway, White Man was
tired, so he laid down and cried "Eyes, eyes, come back, come back!"
But they didn't come back, they just sat there, all the flies buzzing and
sticking to them, you know. He was so tired he started to fall asleep,
and just before he fell asleep a little mouse ran over to him. White
Man closed his eyelids so the mouse wouldn't see that he was blind
The mouse crept up, slowly slowly up onto his face. Like this. You see
the mouse wanted to take some of White Man's long yellow hair for
his nest. Then the mouse licked the tears from White Man's face and
his little tail just sort of slid into White Man's mouth. This is a serious
story with a moral So stop squirming and listen carefully.

(It's funny and disgusting. I think you're making all this up!)

Quiet. Little mouse's tail is in White Man's mouth and what do
you think White Man does? He bites down on its tail and grabs the
mouse, like this, and proceeds to tell it all about his terrible misfortune.
The mouse says in his little squeeky voice: "Yeah, I can see your eyes up
on that branch, they got flies all over them. Pretty disgusting, I'd say
Now you think you could let me go?" "I don't think so." said White
Man. Even though the mouse kvetched and begged, and even offered

to go up the tree and maybe retrieve one of the eyes, White Man said
"NO!" and held on to the mouse even tighter.

(*Oh poor little mouse!*)

The little mouse got tired and said: "Look, what do I have to do
to win my freedom?" White Man said: "I'll only let you go if you give
me one of your eyes so I can see again." "OK," said the mouse, "You
got a deal." And he gave one of his eyes to White Man and ran away
happy to be free again. But the mouse's eye was very tiny and sat way
back in White Man's eye socket like this, so he couldn't see so good.
But he saw far away with his teeny eye, a buffalo grazing in a field,
so he said "This buffido has the power to help me in my trouble." So
he went up to buffalo, walking carefully looking out with his teeny eye
like this, and introduced himself. Buffalo said: "What do you want,
White Man, can't you see I'm having my supper?" White Man told
him he had lost his eye and needed one so he could see again. Buffalo
said "Shpilkes! Why didn't you say so?" And he took out one of his eyes
and gave it to White Man.

(*This gets sillier and sillier. I never heard a mouse or a buffalo talk!*)

That's because you never listened. Now with the buffalo eye White
Man could see far again. But the eye did not fit in the socket, it stuck
way out. So here was White Man with one teeny-weeny eye in one
eye socket and one BIG bulgey eye in the other. And that's the way it
is. And that's the end of the story.

"That's it?"

"Yep! End of story!" He smacked his hands on his knees and
stood up.

"But what's the moral? You said there was a moral!"

"Well, you just have to find it, don't you? That's your job. My
job is to tell the story, your job is to get the moral."

"But ... NO! That's not right! It's *your* story, or Chasing Foxes'
or whoever. *You* have to tell the moral!"

Alonzo shrugged grandly and spread his hands. "That's up
to you. If you can't see the moral all by yourself, then . . ." he
shrugged again. "Well, that's up to you, you just missed the point.

And it's *Watching* Foxes." He smiled until his eyes pinched closed and I fumed with frustration.

"I think it's a dumb story, anyway."

Alonzo dusted off his pants and I handed him his cane. My mind seethed with questions and arguments, but before I could give them voice, a call came rolling through the cricketsong down to where we stood.

"DA! YOHANYA!"

Then joined the fine alto of my grandmother: "Lonzo! Joanna! Come on! Before the skeeters eat you alive!"

We turned and hobbled and marched together like one man short of "The Spirit of Seventy-Six" up to the house and our coffee and pie.

"You're crying."

"No, I'm not. I mean I'm not really crying, just remembering."

We sat in the car looking at what used to be Edgecombe. The house stood empty. Fading "No Trespassing" signs had been nailed up on the doors, the front windows, the post on the front porch and on the old oak, which was showing some signs of decay. The little crooked swing was gone; not even a bit of frayed rope to remind one of where it hung. On the porch the old glider leaned back against the wall, looking surprised and naked without the protective decency of its cushions. In my mind I evoked a picture of the house as it had been: clean and happy and welcoming. I closed my eyes and reopened them, as if to transform it back to its old warmth by an act of will.

"They came back." I opened the door of the car and got out slowly.

"Who?"

I didn't answer but walked slowly towards the house and stopped at the front steps.

"There was a young person whose history
Was always considered a mystery;
She sat in a ditch, although no one knew which,
And composed a small treatise on history."

"The birds. They always come back, no matter what the wind says. They come back to the same place every year. There was a house wren who built a nest in the old privvy. She came back every year and took apart the old nest, piece by piece. Then she rebuilt it with whatever she found, including the bits of the old nest she had dismantled." I laughed. "Is that dumb, or is that smart?"

"YES."

"I was sure you'd say that." I walked around to the side of the house, John at my side. "Did you know that birds can play? Oh yes, they do. We had tree swallows that would circle around in the sky, drop a feather, and swoop down and catch it. And then do it over again! Birds are so ... John! Give me a leg up, will you?" We had reached the apple tree outside the parlor window and I decided I wanted to try to find the robin's nest that was always there.

After a scuffle and a great deal of giggling and groping, John lifted me up to where I could grab the lower limb. I made a pert remark and quickly avoided his hand as he grabbed at my foot. I slowly moved to where I remember the nest that Nammy had pointed out to me that fateful summer. The tree was beginning to die. The limb that used to reach towards the house was riddled with the entrance wounds made by insects, beginning their early recycling of the tree. There probably had been no growth or leafing for at least two seasons. The main trunk was still swollen with life and bravely trying to bring forth scrawny new shoots.

"*Poor old thing.*" I thought as I hugged its scabby bark. 'As the apple tree among the trees of the wood, ... How does that go again, John?'

"What?"

"It's from the Bible, I think ... YOU remember! Oh, here it is! It's here!"

"Be careful! I'm not going to catch you if you fall! You're on your own!"

"Did I call you a mensch? I take it back! Ungallant lout!"

I braced my feet and moved out onto the limb I leaned as close as I could and impulsively reached out toward the nest. I had decided that I wanted to take it home with me. With my arm wrapped around the trunk of the tree I managed to reach the small bundle of twigs that had served generations of robins as a home.

"I've got it!"

"Great! Now come on down before you break your neck!"

"YAY!"

"Joanna, you really are going to break your neck!"

"No no! Move over! Here I come!"

I gently put the nest in my jacket pocket. Then I inched my way down to the lower branches and jumped the rest of the way.

"Come on!" I got up and ran around the house to the front porch. Behind me John mumbled something about reverting to childhood and the need for discipline.

I had been deliberately avoiding looking at the house after my first glimpse when we arrived. Gradually, I told myself, gradually look at the remains, the dust and ashes of the past.

We sat down together on the porch steps and began to examine my treasure. How much of what we see and find is our own truth, and I looked at the little nest weaving my own needs into its structure. The found things, opportunistic bits forgotten by their wingless, earthbound hosts: musty, faded strips of fabric (from Nammy's Sunday-go-to-meeting dress, I'm sure), shards of greyed, crisp wood shavings (from the floor of Alonzo's workshop, of course); a shoelace!; and bits of wool. I pulled a bit of the wool out to look at it more closely. Time and weather had purified it; grey and weak, depleted of vibrancy and resiliancy, it fell from my hand a dead thing. Had that been from the sweater Nammy had made and then destroyed in a flare of pain? I poked further, gently stretching the nest a bit and I found another piece of wool, deep in its woven throat. I pulled it out gently. It was short and also without color, but I recognized it: I knew where it came from. I held it up to the sun and smiled.

"Raggedy Ann. This is from my Raggedy Ann!"

"Joanna! How do you know?" John laughed softly. I just smiled and nodded.

"It is. I just know." I turned to him and smiled. "Some things you just know."

We saw Ardath and Cameron off on the train on Monday morning. It was a rather subdued departure, without the usual antics and impertinent remarks of my older cousins. We had all gone along for the ride so the suitcases had to be tied to the roof of the station wagon by yards and yards of clothesline. Ardath had insisted on holding her hat box on her lap. I suspected that it didn't hold a fashionable hat at all but probably some contraband makeup, a book or two, and some other personal junk. She sat with her hands folded primly over the box while Cameron stared silently out of the window. Andrew hummed tunelessly, moving his hands slowly to his silent lyric.

When we arrived at the station, Alonzo and Cameron untied the luggage and brought it to the platform's edge. Nammy handed a shoebox to Cameron and told him there should be plenty to eat and to be sure to share the desert with his sister. He sighed, affected a pained look and told her yes, he would make sure Her Highness got a cookie. Alonzo sat on one of the benches, rocking his cane back and forth on his knees and smoking a cigarette while Andrew ran up and down the length of the platform, hooting and smacking the flank of his invisible horse. The rest of us waited in stilted silence until a lonely far-off cry warned us of the train's imminent arrival. We braced ourselves against its shuddering power as it coughed and gasped up to the platform in an acrid swirl of gritty air.

We counted and recounted the suitcases and exchanged brief hugs. Ardath kissed me quickly on the cheek. It was not one of her usual queenly pecks, but a real kiss, with a soft smacking sound accompanied by an embarassed smile.

"See you next month, Josie!" She waved breezily and turned quickly to mount the steps of the waiting train.

Suddenly Cameron pulled me aside, avoiding the rest of the family and the possibility of being overheard. He looked at me uncomfortably with his wonderful, cool, grey-green eyes and spoke to me quickly in a low voice.

"You're OK, Joanna. It was a really good thing you did." He grinned and swatted me on the arm. "See you later, sweet potata!" And I fell in love with him all over again.

We stopped at the market on the way home to pick up our weekly grocery order. Andy went with Nammy, taking the steps two at a time and then waited to hold the door for her. He had assigned himself the job of carrying the grocery bags for his mother. Once I had offered to help and he explained firmly, small brown hands flying, that "This is a man's work." and smiled indulgently at me, squinting and nodding like a miniature of his father. I rolled down the window and watched as a small squadron of flies buzzed around an old hound asleep on the porch. His ears twitched and his tail flopped softly. The flies regrouped and buzzed around him again, lighting here and there on his pulsing sides. Alonzo flicked his cigarette end out of the window and cleared his throat.

"Got the moral of that story yet, Little One?"

"No."

Silence. He turned to me and smiled almost sadly. "Maybe there isn't one. Maybe the story was just made up for the entertainment of little ones, you know, something with talking animals, and disgusting stuff and all."

"I think there is a moral. I just haven't figured it out yet, that's all." I said with an attempt at pertness.

He smiled and nodded. There was a short pause and he nodded again.

"Your gramma isn't mad at you, you know. She's just afraid that Andy'll get hurt. That's the way momma's are, you know." I didn't know. I maintained a stony silence. He paused and reached in his pocket for another cigarette, retrieved one and stroked it tenderly before putting it between his lips. "You know Andy goes to a special school where they found out he's very smart, they just thought he was dumb because he's deaf, you know. But they have tests, you know. They can give you tests to find out how smart you are."

I was becoming impatient. I always knew Andy was smart. Sometimes grownups could be very slow. "Then why can't he talk? I mean why don't you let him talk? He's smart, he can learn! Dammit, Alonzo!"

He began to laugh, nodding his head and closing his eyes. The laugh ended in a wheeze and he began to cough.

"You shouldn't smoke, Alonzo."

He looked at me down his nose and said seriously: "Then you wouldn't get to make all those homemade cigarettes you kids always fight over making with that little machine. Ha! Think of *that*!" He nodded, eyes wide, and took a deep drag on the cigarette before he threw it out of the window. He continued to nod, smiling softly to himself.

I thought about the brave little contributions we children made toward the war effort: making homemade cigarettes, squashing the orange packet of color into the white margerine with a fork until your arm ached, weeding the victory garden while the mosquitos whined in your ears and stung your arms and neck. It was hard being at war; being told to "conserve", a new word in our vocabulary. The plenty we took for granted had been rationed. I prayed that we would win the war soon so we could have anything and everything we wanted and Alonzo would be able to buy his Lucky Strikes again.

The nasty, bloody calamity that was the Second World War was so foreign to us that the small deprivations that we suffered were regarded as personal affronts. I was unable to comprehend the devastation that was taking place beyond the comfortable shelter of our home.

"When do you think the war will be over, Alonzo?"

He hummed and mumbled a bit, shaking his head. "Don't know, Little One. Maybe go on for a long time. They're fighting everywhere. It's a world war, you know. In Europe, Africa, Asia, everyplace but here." He signed. "People don't never seem to learn, do they?" He shook his head and I suddenly felt terribly sad.

"She thinks maybe they'll laugh at him, you know. Because he talks, when tries to talk, he sounds, like, you know, funny."

"DIFFERENT. He sounds different. It isn't funny. He sounds different. He *is* different. There's nothing wrong with being different! *I'm* different! Goddamn it, Alonzo...!"

"Don't swear, Little One. Your gramma doesn't like it. Don't say that."

He didn't seem to notice that I was crying.

The dog stood up and stretched, scattering his glittering coterie of flies. He sat suddenly with a thump and began to scratch behind his ear. Andy emerged from the store hugging a large bag.

"*I'm* different. I'm selfish and stupid. I let Toby drown because I was selfish! I wanted to swim and play by myself, and he drowned!" Now I was sobbing, my throat and chest torn with pain. I no longer cared what he thought about me, about Andy, about the war, about anything. I just cried and cried.

The waves rushed forward, green-glass sharp and cold, trimmed with crackled lace foam of yellow and white. I ran on sand brown and hard, paved by the soaking sea. Somewhere out there were mermaids and mermen, a silver-green creature with scales of shell, exploding from the ocean where it had lived since before the dawn of time, a bearded giant with the tail of a great golden fish, blowing on a horn of shell the most beautiful, exalting music, calling all sea creatures to sing and celebrate. Into the feral ocean I ran. The waves sucked away from me, taunting, pulling the brown sand from under my heels. Before me a wall of blue-green rose, laughing, grabbing, screaming, roaring, and I turned quickly as a bowl of crystal salt-white burst around my head, drowning all the sounds of the earth, singing all the sounds of the sea. I was flying, flying with the sailfish and the gulls and the clouds and the light. The world was exploding with joy.

Andy had tried to cheer me up as we rode home. He struggled to make me laugh, pulling his mouth wide with his fingers, crossing his eyes and wagging his tongue at me. I wanted him to stop but he just wouldn't give up. He made his voice very tiny "Yohanya! Ah see oo!" and peered through his fingers at me.

"Enough, Andy. That's enough." Nammy signed to him that I wasn't feeling good and that he should be quiet.

He obliged, looking at me soberly out of the corners of his eyes. I almost felt like smiling. Andy was tough.

When we were back at Edgecombe I immediately jumped out of the car and went straight to my room. I knew where I wasn't wanted. I would go away and never cause any more trouble for anyone, ever. Not ever, ever! I opened my suitcase and began throwing things into it until there was a messy pile overflowing and falling out onto the floor. "Why do I always do everything wrong?" I shouted at the picture on the wall, the spider shivering in her web, the swallow's empty nest, the slanting sunlight, everything, nothing. "I want to do right! But something always happens!" My grief had withered and in its place was an angry self-pity that looked down a tunnel of dim shadow.

A call bounced up the stairwell interrupting my thoughts and delivering a painful shock to my chest.

"Joanna! Come on down. I need your help with dinner."

There was a preemptory note in Nammy's voice, something more than a summons to assist in the kitchen. I knew immediately that she wanted "to have a little talk with me." When grownups wanted to have-a-little-talk with you they meant business. Something serious, or unpleasant. Or it could be just another boring reminder to mind our manners and do-as-you're-told. But I had been bad. This might be a BIG talk. I had a moment of panic when I considered the real possibility of being sent away and never being able to come back again. I felt sick as I lowered the lid of my suitcase, which wouldn't close, so I just turned and walked slowly down the stairs, one step at a time.

At the bottom of the stairs, I peered around, looking for someone, steeling myself for another confrontation, another bout of pain. There was silence but for the throaty ticking of the hall clock, which never kept the proper time, but ticked away faithfully, chiming willy-nilly, turning brassy gears and chuffing the quarter hours cheerfully. I walked to the front door and looked out across the yard.

"I'm out here, Joanna. Go get an apron on and come on out."

I did as I was bidden and sat down on the chair beside her. She was shelling peas into a colander. She didn't look up.

"I think it's time to have a little talk, Joanna."

I reached into the paper bag for a handful of the plump smiling pods and dumped them into my lap.

"Alonzo was very upset this afternoon. He thinks he made you unhappy. Made you cry. I tried to tell him it isn't to do with him." She paused and looked up, staring across the lawn. I looked down and pressed a pod until it popped. I spilled the peas, watching them dance into the colander in Nammy's lap.

"Joanna…"she began, and fell silent.

We worked for a while, peeling the pods apart and pushing the bright peas out, pinging and popping into the colander.

Nammy finally paused and leaned back in the rocker.

"Joanna," she began again "you are not responsible for Toby drowning. It wasn't your fault. It wasn't *anybody's* fault." There was a pause. "It just happened." She lowered her head and for an awful moment I thought she was going to cry. I was surprised when she turned to me and smiled.

"You were sad when he died. We were all sad. But you have to put sadness away, sooner or later. Stop thinking about it. *Try* to stop thinking about it." She looked at me for a moment as if deciding what she should say next. The declining sun made a halo around her hair which sprang disobediently away from her carefully pinned bun like filaments of silver and weightless gosling down. She selected another pod with exaggerated care and examined it for a moment.

"Your mother is not a strong person. She was never a strong person. It's sad, but it happens to people sometimes. If she blamed you, she did it because she was grieving, so she wouldn't feel responsible herself. She's still grieving. She'll always be grieving."

As Nammy struggled for words I felt the need to talk, to comfort her, to try to explain. I needed to be understood, even if they got mad at me all over again. I stood awkwardly and untied my apron. Some things I didn't need to explain to her. She knew that I was jealous of Toby when he was born. I remember how she smiled sadly at my anger and tears when I told her that I wished he had never been born. She knew. She understood and made me feel better about my childish jealousy.

"Nammy, what can you do when you are being punished because you have done something very, very wicked? Or at least something that you and everybody thinks is very very wicked?"

She reached up and grabbed my hands. "You didn't do anything wicked, Joanna, I'm trying to tell you that. You have to believe me!" She began to cry softly.

There is a celebrity attached to those suffering. At first one is watched with cautious curiosity. They speak in low voices. Then they turn toward the sufferer, then turn away, like a clumsy sarabande. There is a primal, visceral fear that arises even in the most enlightened; a fear of contagion by the unlucky, the jinxed, the cursed of the gods. They bring casseroles and flowers, then fade away, the angry gods appeased by their offerings. They murmur a prayer of relief that is not their pain, their loss, their grief. Then there comes the solemn withdrawal, their need to distance themselves, uncomfortable with their pity. And still there abides with the griever a silent incubus that takes joy and replaces it with dark, ugly guilt and empty, reverberating silence. I had come to believe this after many years of lonely searching. I needed to survive and I couldn't bear the guilt of my irreparable sin.

I waited while she blew her nose and began rocking back and forth rapidly.

"Nammy?" I said quietly. She nodded, but didn't look at me. I sat down beside her and dragged my chair closer. I wanted to hug her but dared not. That intimacy would be too disarming, too heavy with unspoken expectations or cowardly misunderstandings. No. We saved hugs for the most superficial occasions (although I had in past disobeyed this family dictum) and were expected to be fleetingly brief, with a minimum of physical contact.

"I have something to say." I finally added, without the first idea of where I should begin. I took the colander from her lap and began to shake the peas gently.

"Why do they say 'alike as two peas in a pod'?" I asked. "Look. They're not all the same. This one even has a little white curl on it, like a Kewpie doll. And this one. Look how tiny it is!" I was digging into the peas and watching them slide through my fingers and drop back with soft pops into the collander.

"Like every wise saying it's just sort-of-right. Not *really* true. Nothing is exactly alike. I mean everything is different." Nammy mused.

I jumped in quickly before I lost my courage. "That's right! That's what I mean! I am different. *Andy's* different. People look at us and think we're strange, but maybe it's them that's strange! When Andy grows up maybe he'll want to teach people to…" I trailed off, not quite sure whether to keep on talking, aware as I was now of her fear for her young son. She remained silent so I took a deep breath and continued.

"Andy asked me to teach him to talk. I thought it was a good idea and he is so smart, I figured he could to it, with some help, you know. He worked so hard learning to make sounds like we make. He reads alot and sometimes he reads out loud, too, so he can practice his talking." I hurried on, afraid to stop, reinforcing my belief that the miracle is possible. I needed that confirmation, and if it didn't come from someone else, I would rationalize and justify myself until the cows came home.

The sun emerged from behind a cloud and the leaves of our sheltering sugar maple quivered with pleasure at its reappearance, and applauded with the rising breeze. A bluejay belled and from high above, a skein of wild geese sounded an alarm for the change of season.

"I never wanted to make you feel bad, Nammy." It took a very strong act of will to bring me so close to this place of hurt and fear that I couldn't really understand. "I …. we thought you'd be pleased." I held my breath. Nammy reached for my hand and held it for a long silent moment.

She looked up at me at last and smiled.

"Forgive me, Joanna. I have been so protected up here, insulated from that awful world where people hurt each other so much, that I sometimes forget that we are all in the middle of life. And we should *participate* in it, without fear. But, you know, it isn't easy. Did I say something funny?"

"Just now you sounded just like Alonzo." I leaned forward, grinning and nodding, squirting my eyes. I hollowed and deepened my voice: "That's right, little one, you know? Heap big Indian saying, you know? Don't be *meshugga*, you know?"

She laughed heartily and shook her head. "Joanna, you are a one! You change the subject, you make the jokes. You are impertinent!" She continued to laugh. "I feel sorry for the nuns, trying to fit my incorrigible darling Joanna into their round holes!" We laughed and laughed; the sun and trees laughed with us and we rocked back and forth in our rockers until we ran out of laughing. We rocked silently for a while and I wondered why we had to stop. Where was the end of joy, sorrow, anger? We must have compartments in us, I decided, where we store our laughter, our tears, our rage, and when we use them up, we have to wait for them to fill up again. Happiness, anger, fear, they all return to visit everyone. I looked up through the leaves as they swirled and waved at us.

"You know what?" I finally broke the silence in as low a voice as I could manage so as not to disturb the gentle atmosphere that wrapped us around. "Andy said he would be my brother, since I don't have a little brother anymore."

Nammy didn't reply. A hawk whistled down the wind and we both lifted our heads and shaded our eyes to follow his upward spiral. Suddenly she sat straight and cocked her head at me.

"I'm going to tell you something, Joanna. You're old enough to understand. And I think I owe it to you to, to…" she groped for words. "…to tell you about, AH!" She finished and shook her head in exasperation. With a wave of her hands, she began.

I was my father's favorite, I know that. There is no reason that I can think of, but sometimes it just happens. Something makes you a specially loved child, and I was your Great-grandfather Ashburn's favorite. Cliff was, well, Cliff. He is good, and patient, and I don't think he was jealous at all. Cora, I'm afraid, felt at a disadvantage, and we had what was best called an uneasy truce. My father was painfully aware of Cora's least-favored status and tried very hard to make it up to her.

I didn't want to go to college. I'm afraid I was awfully spoiled. Cora was the beneficiary of my intellectual laziness and was sent to France to study, which is where she met your Great Aunt Evelyn.

(I'm wandering. Sorry.) Finally, Mother and Father put their foot down and said I had to get some education and I decided, without even thinking about it, that I would train to be a nurse. They were disappointed. They felt that it was a bit below what was expected of us to have such a, well, serving profession. I wouldn't budge, and finally they relented and sent me to St. Vincent's in Manhattan, where I took up residence as a nursing student. I don't think I had ever had so much fun in all my life! Going out with other girls, smuggling illegal booze into the dorm, oh it was wonderful! Anyway, I did study, I studied hard, and graduated with honors. It's something I'll always be proud of. I didn't even work for, oh, a year, I think, when my family decided it was time for me to get married. It was expected that I would marry the man who would be your grandfather as soon as I was finished with whatever school they had dragged me thorough, and not imagining any other life and having a less than strong vocation for my chosen profession, I got married. I became Mrs. Arden Chandor.

Nammy had fallen silent. She stopped rocking and looked down at the colander as though it had just magically appeared in her lap. I stopped rocking and waited. She began running her fingers through the shelled peas, softly moving them about in circles. She held up the pea with the little white curl.

"This pea is going to be a mother. This little white thing" she touched it gently "is the beginning of a root. We will put aside Mrs. Kewpie-Doll Pea and plant her in a flower pot before you leave." She held it up, turning it gently in the warmth of the sun. Then she sighed softly and put the pea in her apron pocket.

Your grandfather was the handsomest man I'd ever seen. I was the envy of all the girls of my age, and when he married me there was general mourning among the debutante set. But sometimes you can be too rich and too good-looking. Believe me! At least that was the way it was with Arden. We had three beautiful daughters, rather quickly, and my hands were quite full. I saw less and less of your grandfather as he got more and more involved with the family business. At least that's what I thought he was involved with. I know you're young, Joanna, but I'm sure you know that married people don't always get along as well as they should. After a number of years, I became very unhappy and dissatisfied, and against the strong objections of my mother and father, I went back to nursing. Times are changing, I know. And they're changing for the better. Women just didn't work away from home when they were married. Especially if they didn't need the money. So, I created something of a scandal right then. But I was stubborn. Like you, Joanna. I was working in a hospital in New York when I met Alonzo. He had been injured while working on one of the skyscrapers. They brought him into the emergency suite badly hurt. I've never seen anyone so hurt. They thought he wouldn't live through the night. But he did. And he lived another day, and another, and another. I stayed with him and watched him as he got better. He was an amazing man. He wasn't afraid. He was in terrible pain but he didn't complain. I have never known anyone like him. And he could laugh. He didn't know if he'd ever walk again, but he still made people laugh. I stayed with him. Sometimes I stayed through two shifts, falling asleep in the chair by his bed. I fell in love with him. I, a married woman, from a good family, fell in love with an Indian, a savage. I committed the unpardonable sin, and as it turns out, it was the only lever that they could use for our divorce. Alonzo and I have never committed any, what they call 'impropriety', we couldn't. The poor man was so disabled that he had trouble feeding himself. But the taint was there, and I found myself disgraced, divorced and a virtual outcast. We lived for a while with Mother and Father, "for the children's sake, you know" and grew more and more unhappy. It was simply awful. I was almost forty years old and was back home with my parents who couldn't hide their disappointment and disapproval. When your mother and aunts were off to college or working, I think Eleanor had married by then, I left and found a place of my own in the city, where I continued to see Alonzo. He had had some months of rehabilitation and made a remarkable recovery, considering the extent of his injuries. They told him that he would have painful, chronic ailments as he grew older and would probably not live very long. And he would never be able to have children.

Nammy put her head against the back of the chair and laughed.

They were wrong. As you can see. When I found out Andrew was on the way, we went to the Registrar's Office downtown at City Hall, and got married. A negro cleaning lady and an old janitor were our witnesses. We went to the Automat for our wedding breakfast and then went back to our tiny, tiny apartment on the upper west side.

We were very happy. I realized that I hadn't know what it was to be in love. I know it sounds foolish, but it is true.

To make a long story short, we found out through a friend that this old place was available cheap, so we took the plunge and bought it with the paltry disability settlement Alonzo got and some money I had saved from working.

And that's what happened. I guess it doesn't sound very exciting, but I thought maybe you were curious about why we're up here, so far away from home and what they call civilization.

We like it here. It's peaceful. And we are accepted on our own terms. Alonzo isn't a savage, I'm not Hester Prynne, and our child is the best little boy that ever there was.

Her voice caught and she stopped speaking. She pressed her fingertips against her lips and sighed deeply.

I remained silent for a while, wanting all the while to jump up and cheer and hug her and spill the peas all over the porch. But a great surge of gratitude for her trust held me fast.

I remained silent for a while, wanting all the while to jump up and cheer and hug her and spill peas all over the porch. But a great surge of gratitude for her trust held me fast.

"Well, there it is!" She turned to me and smiled, clapping her hands together.

"Who is Hester Prynne?" I asked.

Nammy laughed. "She is a woman in a book called 'The Scarlet Letter'. You should read it when you get a little older. Add it to your list!" she commanded. "That list of all the books you should read, and cherish, and reread. You know a wise man once said 'The man who doesn't read has no advantage over one who cannot.' And he was right!"

I wanted this moment to go on forever. The ambience of the day, the weather with its cool suggestion of summer's end, the birdsongs, the smell of something baking in the summer kitchen, the overgrown garden and the hollow where Trot had carved himself a hard, dusty bed in a patch of coneflowers and phlox.

A hooting call bounced up the yard announcing the approach of Alonzo and Andy.

"The intrepid fishermen return with their catch!" Nammy said happily and she answered their calls with a yoohoo and a wave.

She cupped her hands around her mouth and called" "Don't come back without checking the corn! See if there's any left for tonight!" She stood and signed her message twice, nodding and calling "Corn! Corn!"

I saw Andy hand his stringer to his father and turn to race away while Alonzo rocked slowly up the lawn, leaning on his cane and holding the fish with his free hand. He was panting when he reached the porch.

"Should have brought the creel, you know? Didn't think we'd get so many fish! Lookit that!" He held up the stringers triumphantly, smiling and breathing heavily. The fish glittered and shone with slick flashes of silver. Occasionally one twitched and jerked, then stretched still in the drowning air.

"You know the rules." Nammy said firmly. "You catch 'em, you clean 'em!" Alonzo nodded and recited the rule along with her.

"I'll help!" I was jumping up and down. Ordinarily I hated cleaning fish, but today it didn't seem like such a chore after all.

"OK, little one. But remember, you have to give thanks to the God of the Pond, you know. Oh, yes!" He nodded and winked at Nammy who shook her head and cast her eyes heavenward.

He raised his arm, put his head back and closed his eyes. I heard Nammy murmur as she went into the house. "You're crazy, 'Lonzo. You must have fallen on your head when you went off of that building."

Alonzo seemed oblivious, in a trance. He began to hum, then chant. Then he shouted. I jumped, startled.

"Oh, great spirit of the pond, we thank you for your offerings of crappies for our meal. And we hope you will continue to provide bounty for your table. It would be nice, though, if you could see it clear to let me catch that landlocked salmon that legend tells us, lives in our pond. Now *that* would be good. That would be *real* good! In the meantime, many, many thanks from the children of earth's man-tribe for your generosity and your continued patience with a *momzer* like me." Then he hummed some more, slowly lowered his arm, opened his eyes and winked at me.

I smiled. "I got it, Alonzo. I *think* I got it." I smiled and nodded. "You know?"

"What's that, little one?" he mounted the steps painfully and headed for the summer kitchen where he dumped their catch into the laundry tub for cleaning.

I followed him bouncing and leaping back and forth. "I'm *sure* I got it!"

He ran water over the fish and washed his hands. "OH kay!" Let's hear it!" He turned and walked back out to the porch and heaved down onto the glider that let out a long whoosh of air.

"See, white man, he doesn't listen, you know? He thinks he knows everything!" Alonzo was nodding and bouncing gently on the glider.

"So, when he couldn't get his eyes back, he gets eyes from a mouse and a buffalo and they don't fit! So, he sees everything coocoo, you know, all *wrong!*" I struggled to make myself clear. I jumped up and down, thrashing my arms. "Like, *FARPTCHKIT!* You know?" He started to chuckle.

"You know, Little One, I think that's as good an interpretation as any *I've* ever heard. When you tell it to your kids, be sure that you tell them that Alonzo Two-Feathers, the wise old indian, told you that story and it changed your life!" He laughed, I laughed, and we turned to hear Andy laugh, as he ran towards us from the garden with the old wicker creel filled with corn, tasseled and golden in the sun

We sat on the old glider, which, after having been tested, proved to still be strong enough to bear our weight. A moth-eaten lap robe fetched from the trunk and John's windbreaker made a serviceable improvised cushion. I had finished my narration and was musing through a new spate of memories which had percolated out of my subconscious like freshets into an old stream bed or the silken, spangled milkweed down that had always eluded my dreamcatcher. The view from the porch had reawakened the child in me, and with shock I realized that I was still that child: still questing, still impatient, waiting for answers and dissatisfied with them when they came. I sighed more with resignation than relief.

John spoke musingly. "So, you could say there is a sort of a happy ending but you didn't really live happily-ever-after."

"You could say that." I rejoined. "I still dream about Toby, sometimes, and I wake with a sort of bleak feeling. I'm not sure it'll ever go away, but the pain has been dulled. I know in my head that his death wasn't my fault. But my viscera still feeds my old Calvinistic conscience. I know. But I'm still looking. Still trying."

"I love you." he said.

I reached for his hand.

"Me too!"

We moved toward each other. The glider gave a muffled screech and something popped deep in its scrawny gut. Saying goodbye to something else, I thought. I won't go back into the house. At least not this time. A swallow swooped past and glinted peacock-blue wings at us. I am sure it is the child of the child of the child of my swallow, who kept me company in the tiny attic room.